Benedict Kiely was born in 1919 near Dromore, Co. Tyrone. He grew up and went to school in Omagh and is a Freeman of that town. Apart from some years in the United States, most of his life has been spent in Dublin. He graduated from University College, Dublin and worked as a journalist, broadcaster and lecturer. He is past-president of the Irish Academy of Letters. His first book of memoirs *Drink To The Bird* will be published by Methuen in 1991.

LAND WITHOUT STARS

By the same author

NOVELS

In a Harbour Green
Call for a Miracle
Honey Seems Bitter
There Was an Ancient House
The Cards of the Gambler
The Captain with the Whiskers
Dogs enjoy the Morning
Proxopera
Nothing Happens in Carmincross

SHORT STORIES

A Journey to The Seven Streams
A Ball of Malt and Madame Butterfly
A Cow in the House
A Letter to Peachtree

NON-FICTION

Counties of Contention
Poor Scholar; A Life of William Carleton
Modern Irish Fiction
All the Way to Bantry Bay
Ireland from the Air
Drink to the Bird (forthcoming)

EDITED BY THE SAME AUTHOR

Penquin Book of Irish Short Stories
The Small Oxford Book of Dublin
Yeats' Ireland

Benedict Kiely

LAND WITHOUT STARS

A land without dry weather, without a stream, without a star
Tir gan turadh gan buinne gan reiltean

Egan O'Rahilly

MOYTURA PRESS • DUBLIN

First published in 1946 by
Christopher Johnson Publishers Ltd, London

This edition published in 1990 by
Moytura Press, 3 The Dale, Stillorgan Grove, Co. Dublin.

BRITISH LIBRARY CATALOGUING IN PUBLICATION DATA
Kiely, Benedict *1990-*
Land without stars. — 2nd. ed.
I. Title
823.914 [F]

ISBN 1-871305-04-7

Printed in Ireland by
Betaprint International Ltd, Dublin

To Maureen

Contents

Retrospect

Forty four, or so, years ago when this novel, my first, was published, a lady-reviewer, who lived well down into Munster, said that it was obvious that the author knew nothing about young people in the North of Ireland. Since at that time one of the few things I knew anything about was young people in the North of Ireland. I developed the oddest ideas about lady-reviewers, or just about all reviewers, including myself. Now, the best part of a half-century later, I wonder.

The young people in this novel seem to be so innocent. More innocent, even, than I was when I wrote the book. Was it, then, a more innocent world? Or has the world never been any better or any worse? The young I.R.A men of that time read "Mein Kampf" because Hitler was against England. But their world was still innocent of the full implications and sideshows of the Hitler war, of the revelations of Belsen and Katyn Woods, of Hiroshima, napalm in Viet-Nam, of the Abercorn restaurant, and Derry's Bloody Sunday and Belfast's Bloody Friday, and the Chicago murders, nor of Charley Manson and the slaughter of Sharon Tate.

The moon was still a virgin, that orbéd maiden with white fire laden, and not an ash-heap. Most Irish rivers ran clean. The streets were not constipated with motor-cars. Nor did you inhale carbon monoxide on O'Connell bridge. No, no, nothing worse than the homely body-odour of Anna Livia Plurabella.

"Mein Kampf", by now, is somewhat out of fashion. And the young Provos, if they read at all, read. . . . I know not what. Davy Quinn already knew about handbooks telling you how to blow things up. But it is doubtful if his feelings on his first visit to Dublin, or his simple romanticism about that city, would now be shared by any young fellows. The proliferation of automobiles, with or without bombs, has made Dublin so much more accessible and less desirable. It is doubtful, too, if a young man with even a suspicion of Davy's politics, or religion, would now get any class of a job in the post office in the Six Counties. Because over the intervening years Stormont managed to tamper with the integrity of that then impeccable British socialist institution. It was a relative of mine who said, back in those days, that because he was a British postal offical he was, of, necessity a Socialist. He also was a devotee of Shaw and Wells and Gisssing and "The Ragged-Trousered Philanthropists". And of Ralph Waldo Emerson. Dear God!

The town cinema is not the social centre it was. It's not even safe. And television is with us. And the Back Alley is gone and there are new handsome suburbs. But there are bombed and burnt-out ruins on the High Street.

Rita Keenan's dark skirt would nowadays hardly cover her rump, let alone her knees. Her school of ballroom-dancing and the days when people quickstepped to the jingle of hanging out the washing on the Siegfried line are worlds away from the leaping screaming, somersaulting showbands of today.

Ancient superstitions had lived on into her world: the girl that drew the clerical student away from his calling would never have luck. That, and more, has gone on the wind and even novitiates, I'm told, are not what they were.

Odd things peep out at me as I reread. Pete and Jacob appear more elaborately, and more happily, in a later short story, "Homes on the Mountain", in the collection, "A Journey to the Seven Streams" (Methuen: 1963). The ill-luck, or hard fate of Dick Slevin is, also, that of the eponymous character in the story, "The Wild Boy", in that same collection, but the moral motivation is completely different. Slevin is conscious that he's just a guy who doesn't fit in anywhere while Davy is even more acutely conscious that he is a soldier of the Republic. They may have their counterparts today even if there are only two violent deaths in the whole book: a mere post-prandial trifle in these sad times. Selvin is also aware that he has blood on his hands and, in the row with the stiff-necked ex-celibate, it is the hunted killer who has the last word. What that may mean I'm not quite cetain. Honesty?

That portrait of Slevin drew down on me the disapproval of some young men then rusticating in Crumlin Road Jail. Joseph Tomelty was similarly disappoved of. But their veto, I was told, was vetoed by that sensible man, Hugh Mc Ateer, and two of the vetoers, a fine word, afterwards became firm friends of mine.

Its startles me now to be reminded by my own words how the Second Big War silenced the church bells. Churchill's dismal spires were even more dismal because they were dumb, and the bells were held in reserve either for calamity or final jubilation. It is perhaps, even more startling to be reminded that part of the world did once rejoice for peace or victory, or whatever. West Germany and Japan were not then so jubilant and their economic victory, perhaps the greatest irony of the woeful war was still to come.

That argument in the hotel in West Donegal reminds me, too, that bullshit was talked as plentifully then as now. But today a lot more people die violently in Ireland. And the beauty of Ballyshannon is half-departed, thanks to the Electricity Supply Board. And the Six Counties are more than ever the land without dry weather, without a stream, without a star that the bitter Kerry poet wrote about long ago.

To write a foreward to one's own book, is of course, a sly way of reviewing oneself: forty four years later. Yet the temptation to compare past and present is strong. And I suppose that in our accelarated world, anything becomes history after forty four years. That description of the town on a market-day reads now even to me, like a fragment of William Carleton and, perhaps, I myself am a figment of Carleton's imagination, or he of mine.

In a later story, "Down Then By Derry", to be found in the collection, "A Ball of Malt and Madame Butterfly", (Gollancz: 1973), an exile returned to his native northern town says to some friends: "When I read the newspapers today there are times I think I was reared in the Garden of Eden".

And they answer him: "Weren't we all?"

Thirty years from now a man approaching his middle fifties may feel that way about 1990.

B.K.
Dublin, 1990

1

Christmas Holiday

I

THE brothers came home on the same day. Davy came southwards on the train from Derry, a slow train, dusty box-carriages, half a dozen passengers, the engine creaking breathlessly along from one small station to the next. It crossed and recrossed the great river big and brown with flood-water, torn into white foam at rocky places or around the eyes of bridges. Winter had drained heat and life out of the fields in the valley. The square of trees around each farmhouse stood bare, stripped sentinels, grey and still with frost. The dull sky was low over the valley, covering the tops of the mountains, wreathing the moors and the higher farms with damp mist.

Davy picked his tool-kit off the dusty seat, nodded to the soldier in battledress who sat gloomily in one corner of the carriage. He balanced the kit on his shoulder, buttoned his top-coat with his free hand, passed out of the station. The short December sunlight was gone, the sky hardening with blue frost. A hackney-man nodded to him.

"Home again, Davy."

"Aye."

"How's Glasgow?"

"The same as ever."

"Any sign of war?"

"Soldiers all over the place. Air-raid shelters and sirens. A big push in industry."

"Do the Glasgow people like it?"

"They'll take it. The people always do."

The hackney-man saw a likely customer, excused himself. Davy threaded his way through waiting cars, dodged across the road before the red mail-van, stopped to light a cigarette, then stepped out homewards along the footwalk. The dusk and the frost came together, hardening and blackening the air. No lamps darted to sudden glimmering life in the streets of the town. Dull blue lights shone in shop-windows; heavy curtains draped the doors, crushing in the yellow glow. The darkness had followed him from Glasgow, the great clanging city, mother of ships, where thousands of people waited, tense, sullenly nervous, for the bursting of the storm. All over Europe the same darkness. A broken Poland. Great hordes of men moving east and west. The darkness spreading, west to Ireland, swirling through the streets of the little town, blackening the windows of his own home.

His mother had bought a new black blind. No thin line of light came through to the quiet side-street. He smiled as he put his hand to the knocker, thinking of the careful counting of pennies behind that new purchase.

Peter came an hour later, northwards on the train from Dublin, crossing the broad Boyne, halted at the Border high in the Gap of the North where frost had crusted the snow into crystal hardness. The Customs officer glanced at his black clothes and soft white collar, his case filled with books, courteously made his chalk- mark and passed on. An old lady in the compartment turned her eyes from the great white plain stretching beyond Newry to the half-visible Mourne Mountains. She asked him what college he belonged to.

"Foreign missions," she repeated tenderly. Her eldest boy had gone out two years ago on the Chinese mission The pain of parting. And now the war, the uncertainty of everything. Did he think Japan would come in? He said no, listlessly, that Japan was afraid of the United States. She said she was glad to hear *that* from a student, an educated young man, one in a position to know. He sighed, sinking into silence. People would talk about it just as men would fight in it. They fluttered around the flame, morbidly curious, until the moment of burning and destruction came. The good things of God's universe were forgotten: books, great beauty like the snow-covered plain running into the shadowy mountains.

At Portadown he changed trains, leaving the old lady. Figures in uniform crowded the platforms, vague in gathering shadows under dull blue lights. Far down the train a soldier began to sing. His butties joined him, bellowing in chorus until the train moved and their voices were lost in the shrieking of steam and the clanking of wheels. The carriage was a bubble of blue light crushed in an ocean of darkness, preserving its tiny, frail, pitiful integrity. The faces of the travellers were dull like the faces of corpses. Somewhere to the right was Mullagharn Mountain and the hills of Sperrin, lost in the darkness, inert and heavy in the clench of the frost.

His father met him at the station, lugged his bag to the hired hackney, and they drove home.

II

The family sat down together around the tea-table. Peter sat at the head of the table, blessed himself and said grace out loud.

"Thank God," said Mary, "we've a clerical student in the family. Their way o' saying grace is as good as Father Fahey chanting at Benediction."

She pushed her red hair off her forehead, carefully sugaring her tea. Her father tossed the evening paper into the armchair beside the range and turned to eat.

"It's good to be home again," said Davy. "Glasgow's all right, but, my God, they haven't the grub there we have here. I don't know what they'll eat in three years' time if the war lasts."

"It won't last," said the father.

"It'll last as long as God lets it," said the mother.

Silence except for the tapping of knives and forks, the clink of teacups returning to saucers. The father glowered under heavy eyebrows at his plate, thinking his way back forty or fifty years.

"It's a big change," he said, "since the year they went to South Africa to beat Kruger."

"You went with them, Da," said Davy.

"I never denied it. I was young an' foolish an' many a young fella does a foolish thing. But if I was on the wrong side I never claimed that we were better men than the Boers. They could shoot. Man ! they could shoot. They were as hardy as goats."

"Devout men in their own way," said Peter.

"They were devout an' their way was a good, honest way. De Wett never won a fight without going on his bended knees to thank

Almighty God. Paul was as fond of his bible as he was of his pipe."

"The bible wasn't the book for his game," said Davy, lowering his cup. "The British had handbooks of military strategy. That was how they won. What Kruger wanted was a wee book on revolutionary method. How to blow up things."

"Up the republic," mocked the red-headed sister.

"Davy thinks Alexander an' Caesar were only in the ha'penny place compared with Sean Russell."

"By God, but he put the wind up the English anyway. He let them know that Ireland unfree and partitioned would never be at peace."

"The I.R.A. are antagonistic to both Church and State," said Peter. "The two things that . . ."

"Listen to him. Listen to the future bishop. If that's the kinda stuff they feed you on in college . .. "

"Now, Davy," said the mother, blinking her pale eyes. "That's no talk in the holy Christmas season. More tea, Mary? Reach the pot from the hob behind you, Daddy."

After tea Jack Carney called for Mary. He draped his overcoat and scarf on the banister of the narrow, twisting stairway that went up out of the kitchen. He sat down by the fire.

"You're looking well, Peter," he said. "They feed you in that place."

"That's all they have to do," grunted Davy, kneeling on the mat at the bottom of the stairs to polish his shoes.

"Old Davy still," said Carney. "Davy Quinn, radical, revolutionary and Irish republican."

"You're a nice one to talk. When my sister's mother wasn't listening to you, you told me that the very fact that you belonged to the Union of Postal Workers made you a socialist."

"Don't mind him, Jack," said old Quinn, touching the flame of a match to his pipe. Jack laughed.

"I don't. We were at school together. He hasn't changed."

In the pantry opening off the kitchen Mary and her mother washed the tea things, swish of warm water, the clink of delph, soft joking voices of the women. Davy shuffled on stockinged feet up the stairs to dress himself for going out. Jack and the father talked idly across the fire, the gossip of the town, the post office, deliveries, mail-vans, the effect the war would have on the Christmas rush. Peter took a book from the press in the corner. Above the press the red lamp burned under the picture of the Sacred Heart. Idly he turned the leaves of the book. Davy's name was scrawled on the fly-leaf; underneath his name Davy had written in a stiff, spidery hand: *This book was bought in Dublin in the August of 1937.* That had been Davy's one visit to Dublin. Peter remembered the occasion clearly: the talk afterwards, the excited descriptions; the crowd coming out of a church on the quays in the bright Dublin sunshine; the water of the Liffey twisted with the wind and the incoming tide; across the river the Four Courts and the flag above the dome; the tricolour, flapping, folding and unfolding. The flag of the Republic. The parade of troops through the streets, active young men in green uniforms; the British would miss them in the next war. The sound of Irish spoken in theatres, cinemas, at dances, football games, in buses, in the streets. Croke Park where thousands sang the National Anthem while the footballers or hurlers stood straight and strong on the green field. . . . Poor Davy. The book was: *The Principles of Freedom.* Would he ever learn?

In the blood, Peter supposed. He glanced under drooping eyelids at his father, stout, bald, red-faced, remembering the pipe of Kruger, the prayers of De Wett, the sharpshooting of tough South African farmers. The old man had got on the wrong side, worn what he considered the wrong uniform, then settled down to a life of bitter memories, risky, bitter words. Risky. After all, he was a postman on His Majesty's service. Yet in some swampy meadow quiet between hills he had once trained young fellows in the use of guns. That was in the fighting days, the days of trouble when the names of some ordinary young men had grown into legends—Collins, De Valera, Cathal Brugha. No logicality. Draw the King's money and plot against the King's Government. A man must earn his bread, marry, bring up children; but there was no suppressing that force and power in the blood, that inherited hatred. Davy didn't lick it off the grass.

The two women came back to the kitchen. Mary stood behind Jack's chair running her hands along his shoulders. He leaned his dark head back against her body, smiling with the easy content of a man sure of his own heart and of the heart of a woman.

"Mrs. Quinn, have I permission to take your daughter to the pictures?"

"What's on, Jack?"

"*The Garden of the Moon*, in the Pantheon."

"It sounds all right."

"Reminds me of the Queen of Sheba," said Peter.

"Don't know what under God takes so many people to the pictures nowadays," said the father. "The picture-loving public. When I was a lad. . ."

"There weren't any movies, Daddy," said Mary.

"We managed to amuse ourselves all the same. Now they go out of the Back Alley with their babies in their arms. Declare to God they don't have the price of their breakfast the next morning."

"Would you grudge them the escape from the Back Alley?" asked Peter.

"It's their own fault they're in the Alley," said Mrs. Quinn. "That brood of tinkers."

"Still, if a wandering tramp came to the door, Mother, you'd give him a penny," said Peter.

"My mother did it before me. She gave for the love of God and His Mother who were without a roof to cover them."

"Get ready, Mary," whispered Carney. "Maybe you'd like to come along, Peter."

"Two's company."

"We don't mind. Except your father and mother want to have you for the night."

"Go, Peter dear," said the mother. "It'll lift your mind from the books."

"Go where?" asked Davy, back again in the kitchen, fastening a clean collar around a short, muscled neck.

"To the pictures."

Davy gripped a comb, ran it carefully through his stiff brown hair, twisting the lips of his square face mechanically, watching with interest the twist reflected in the mirror.

"He oughta come with me. To the Irish class. Fit him better to be learning his own native language than feeding his mind on the tripe from Hollywood."

"Off again," said Jack.

"Well, what I say is the clergy are the leaders in this country. The people look up to them. An' if the clergy don't stand by the language, who will?"

"We don't need Gaelic on the foreign missions."

"Don't need it? That's the mentality for you. That's what the civil servants say in Dublin when they have the jobs. Back to English. We don't need Irish any more. But your native language is a good in itself."

"You must have been reading Newman."

"Newman was an Englishman."

"Pay no attention to him, Peter," said Mary, appearing at the door of her bedroom that opened off the kitchen. "He went last summer to the Rosses of Donegal an' the sea wind isn't out of him yet."

She poked Davy playfully where an inch of white shirt showed between his trousers and waistcoat. He turned, laughing, reaching for her long red hair.

"Mary, you look killin'. Where did you get the coat?"

"A new one. Peter Keyes the tailor made it." He fingered the tweed cloth, then held her at arms' length, suddenly proud of her shapeliness, the fair, oval face, the hair alive with the glint and glimmer of light.

"Poor Jack," he said, "he hasn't a chance to escape."

"He doesn't want one."

"Sweet nineteen," said Davy. "Here, take her, Peter, an' give her some good advice."

III

Davy walked with them as far as the first street corner. They stepped out of the bright kitchen into darkness that weighed on the eyes, heavy and cold. No lights from the windows, no lamps in the streets, no moon. Devlin Street might have been a tunnel in a disused, forgotten mine, the sky pressing down like dark crumbling earth, blotting out the outlines of the houses. Davy shone a pocket-torch now and again, searching with the finger of light for the treacherous edge of the footpath.

He grumbled: "No sense in it at all. Not here. Now you wouldn't mind in England or Scotland. But under God what self-respecting German, would bomb this place? He wouldn't have much to crow about back in the beer-garden."

"Necessary precautions," said Peter.

"Necessary me eye."

He circled around a loaded lorry, parked without light at the edge of the footpath. "An' the way these assassins leave their lorries. Without even a red light. Call that a necessary precaution? It's a greater menace than air-raids. Knew a poor unfortunate who walked smack into a parked lorry loaded with timber. Didn't leave him any face worth talking about."

At the corner of Devlin Street and Dublin Street he left them, giving the pocket-torch to Mary, sardonically advising Peter to leave the cinema if the picture was immoral.

"Let the clergy give good example to the laity. Jack Carney wouldn't know the difference between moral and immoral. They'd all be alike in his Red Republic."

He strode off laughing into the darkness. Through Dublin Street into Courthouse Diamond they talked about him: Peter, solicitous, worried about violent opinions, the danger of the times; Mary, solicitous but trustful; Jack, scoffing at Peter's fears, laughing the violence of Davy into a wordy harmless pose. From the Diamond they went down the sloping Main Street to the Pantheon Cinema. Shadowy soldiers, shadowy civilians crowded around the door, patient in a long queue in the dimness of a blue-lighted lounge. They took their places. At the ticket-office two girls waited, carrying on a broken conversation with the girl behind the glass. They turned to greet Mary; they saw Peter, shook hands with him.

"Welcome home, Peter."

"Thanks, Rita."

"Rita, why aren't you at the Irish class?" Mary asked. "Davy polished himself for half an hour before he went."

The thin, dark girl didn't answer. She looked down under half-closed eyelids, quietly, tensely, thinking. There was a hardness in the outline of her face that banished prettiness, banished even beauty, left instead the suggestion of some restrained force, sharp and delicate, a straining steel spring, a bent sword-blade. She was as tall as Mary, as shapely. She said to Peter:

"Sister Mary is having her little joke, Peter."

"She's always having them."

"Her latest is that Davy has fallen foul of my charms."

"Why shouldn't he?"

"That's a daring thing for a clerical student to say. But it isn't true. It's Mary's imagination. Davy has more sense."

"Sense?"
"Besides I could never keep up to Davy's idealism. I like a quiet life."
"Idealism raises us."
"It raises some of us too high. Higher than God ever meant us to go."
There was a coldness in her voice, neither hostility nor anger. Mary, looking at Peter, wondered at the dead quietness of his face, at his slow picking and deliberate placing of his words. He said: "Nothing could be higher than what God wishes for us."
"Is it the will of God, or our own power to kid ourselves? How do we know?"
"Maybe we don't. We take things on trust."
"Thank God, Jack," said Mary. "You've come in time to stop a theological argument. Rita here should have been a nun."
Jack rattled a handful of change into his pocket.
"Come on. Move. If we want to get good seats. "Coming in, Rita?"
"No, thanks, Jack. We promised to wait on Kitty Smith."
"Righto. But don't sit on my knee when you're hunting for seats in the dark."
They went laughing up soft-carpeted stairs. Mary clattered : "God knows Rita Keenan is a strange girl. Still waters. She was always like that. Even at school you never knew what she was thinking."
Peter was silent, following the usherette's lamp through scented darkness, his feet sinking silently into deep carpet. His mind was numb, gripped by the darkness, cold in the streets, warm in the cinema. He had a strange feeling that the sun would never rise again, that his life had whirled off into night, lit by faint memories of a sunlit world.
The picture wasn't about the Queen of Sheba. The garden wasn't a secret place, scented trees, silent, radiant birds, lithe beauty half-hidden in sleek shrubbery. It was a dance-hall in some American city, any American city. A petty, trivial story, incident after incident dripping like water drops from a leaky tap. A background for the ears, wailing dance-bands, drummer smiling weakly over his drums, gesticulating singers. He sat in bored patience. Mary and Jack had forgotten him, forgotten the picture.

They sat hand in hand, her head resting on his shoulder. He felt suddenly in that attentive darkness the love between them. Some of the chaps in college would be slightly shocked by his awareness. The prospective perpetual celibate. He knew the sort; good fellows, as clean as new snow. They came out of sheltered homes, good schools, straight to the Church, living and dying in a flame of purity, the clean of heart. Their temptations were not like the temptations of other men. Their innocence was half ignorance. They knew the revolt of their own bodies and they resisted, praying, trusting in the Mother of God. But no one had ever told them the reasons behind the revolt.

Well, they didn't lose much. To be good it wasn't necessary to have had the experience of evil. Rolling in the mud might, by the sheer force of contrast, eventually increase one's appreciation of clean air and the sun, but it wasn't an essential condition. Celibacy was still the strange flower growing in the garden of God, white, pure, cold to the touch. Beside him in the darkness was the bud of red blossom, the general lot, ranks upon ranks of red bloom, here and there the exceptional white flower. The red flower was the force of revolt, trained, directed, sanctified, made life-giving by the wisdom and power of God.

Did Jack see it that way or the lovely red-headed girl, his own sister? It wasn't likely. They would be content with feeling, not troubling to define, not troubling even to discuss except in words that babbled and caressed like the waters of a young stream. One hand in another and a lightness behind the ribs. The beating of the blood, the pleasant, spinning emptiness of the mind. The rose and the lily, deep vermilion of the rose, red rose, proud rose, sad rose, nor did I wonder at the lily's white. Poetic symbols that satisfied because they made it easier for men not to understand but to think they understood. A flower fallen from the budded coronal of spring, the bud of the red flower, fallen and trampled. Lorenzo Valla writing his clear, sharp, blasphemous Rennaissance Latin had preferred the fallen flower, his *scorta et prostibula* that deserved better of the human race than the maidens who walked holy, unsullied and clean. No accounting for tastes. But poor, mad Valla had plainly never understood the story of Mary Magdalen. . . .

The picture ended suddenly. The lights went on. People were rising, struggling into coats. A stout woman in the seat before him smoothed the wrinkles in her skirt with a fat, placid hand. A hidden loudspeaker brayed music.

"That's *The King*," Jack said, "they play it for the soldiers since the war began."

"That's why Davy stopped going to the pictures," said Mary.

Davy. The plain, direct Davy, forcible, firm as his handshake, the honest glance of his eyes. Davy regarded his brother as the model clerical student, pious, smooth-spoken, unruffled. Davy could know nothing of the turning and twisting of any mind that did not like his own leap to conclusions, accept shibboleths, simplify life to a struggle between Right and Might, the valiant Green against the mighty Red. For Davy, Prussian boots covered feet beautiful upon the mountains. His own personal problems were lost in great generalisations, unsolved, unsolvable. Davy and Rita Keenan? Why, they had nothing in common, and love needed a foundation somewhere. Even the peculiar case of the Spratt family posited an initial agreement upon the necessity of eating something, fat or lean.

Outside the cinema he shook himself out of thought, talked lightly, easily with Jack Carney about war, school-days, books, pictures. He went in first, leaving the couple chatting in the street. His father and mother had gone to bed. Mary came in laughing, flushed, listening to the footsteps of her man fading down the dark street. She made supper.

By candlelight at his bedside he prayed carefully, reading from his missal the solemn, musical words of a psalm. "Elegi abjectus esse in domo Dei mei: magis quam habitare in tabernaculis peccatorum." To be despised in the house of God. To dwell in the tents of sinners.

Between sleeping and waking he was troubled by a vision of sunlit fields; tossing, blossoming, singing branches and the gleam of white tent-canvas. The sun faded and the fields were dark streets where the poisoned ideas of Valla took flesh and walked, strutting, swaggering, swaying, turning evil, painted faces upwards.

Davy came in after midnight, bolted the door in cautious silence, made and drank a cup of hot cocoa. Then, crouched over the fire, he opened a parcel he had carried in with him, drew from an oily holster a heavy service revolver. He held it on the flat of his hand, turning it slowly, watching the firelight reflected from the blue barrel. He fingered the three-inch fragment of whipcord dangling from the grip. Slashed, pinched from some drunken bobby. God, but it was easy to get the real stuff nowadays. He posed before the mirror, pointing the revolver, smiling at himself down the levelled barrel. Under the tiny wardrobe in his bedroom he raised a loose board, hid the parcel carefully. He thought: if the worst came to the worst he could always strike a blow. He turned in his creaking bed, drew up his knees for balance, and fell asleep.

IV

Eight years previously Saturday morning had meant no school, sleeping until ten or eleven o'clock, coming out of sleep to the noises of a town already awake, somewhere a hammer tinkling on an anvil, the morning sun soaking through thin white curtains, the rattle of farmcarts going up the street to the creamery, dancing jingling cans, warm splashing milk. The creamery was closed now. Two miles below the town a new factory sucked the cows of the country dry, turned out hundreds of shiny tins filled with white powder; for the emergency, for the troops. No morning sun came soaking through the curtains. The black blind shut out the light. He sat up in his bed, reached sideways until he found the tassel, let up the blind with a snap. Light flooded in on him, sudden and dazzling. Davy in the next room called softly.

"Peter, do you hear the guns?"

"Guns?"

"Surely to God. Listen. They woke me up at all hours."

Peter lay listening. From below the town, the flat plain beyond the barracks, he heard suddenly the heavy boom of big guns, then the nervous rattle of machine-gun fire. Davy was rising, the bed creaking and complaining under him. He said: "They're never done practising. Keeps the wee Tommies amused. But damn the bit good it'll do them. Sure you couldn't make soldiers outa the craythers of Englishmen they're conscripting nowadays."

His voice was muffled in his shirt. The guns sounded again. The sound of frying, smell of bacon came from the kitchen up the twisted stairs, seeped into the bedroom. Davy called: "Get up, you lazy monk. Is that what they teach you in college? The saints of God rejoice in their beds while the British soldiers are out learning to kill their fellow men.

"You didn't get up until you smelt the bacon."

Peter dressed himself carefully. His mother had left him the best bedroom, to the front of the house, windows looking out over the town, beyond the town to round, blue mountains. He saw it all in the morning light under the frosty sun, the main street ploughing a furrow between tumbled uneven roofs, the domes on the courthouse and town hall, the blank roof of the new cinema. To the left, barely visible, the tall, imitation Gothic spires of the Catholic church, dwarfing, dominating the plain steeple of a Protestant church. The view from that window was painted in colour on the back wall of his mind. He could close his eyes in any place, at any time, and see it. The low hills around the meeting of two rivers where the town had grown. The sloping land beyond Ballyclogher, a patchwork of fields, going up to the lower slopes of the mountains, coarse, tangled, wiry grass, rough heather. The round valley was the cradle that had nursed him.

He brushed his hair before the mirror. Black hair. Strange that Mary was the only red-headed one in the family, the bird that had slipped out of the bush, a throwback to some grandmother or great-grandmother. His father had been dark when he had been anything, his mother an undefined colour, between black and brown. His mother. . .

She was laying the table in the kitchen, carefully placing plates, saucers, knives, forks on a clean white cloth. A boiling kettle bubbled on the range, smell of cooked rashers from the oven.

"Where's Mary?" Davy asked.

"Gone to work. It's ten o'clock."

"You should have called me for Mass, Mother," said Peter.

"Rest yourself, son. The morning was cold an' the ground was slippery when your father was going out on the delivery. Anyway they call you so early in the college that a rest'll do you no harm."

"He wants to give good example to the like o' me," said Davy, spearing an inch of sausage with his fork.

"How's Mary getting on in the shop?"

"Well enough, Peter. Well enough. The boss, that's the young Mr. Norris, likes her. Even if they are Protestants they're decent. Some of them are better than your own. Anyway Mary will soon be stopping work. Will you like to see her married, Peter?'

"She's getting a good man."

"He's all right," Davy grunted.

"Still, a mother doesn't like to see her only daughter going."

Mrs. Quinn sat for a moment to rest, folding her thin hands, looking steadily at the red glow where flames swelled and burst like bubbles in the heart of the range.

"You don't lose her, Mother," Peter said. "You gain a son."

"Haven't I two sons? Not that Jack isn't a decent lad. An' his father an' mother are the best people walking. Still, it's the beginning of the break-up in the home."

"I began it," said Peter.

"Not you, son. That was the call of God. He needs priests, good priests."

"He needs married couples," said Davy, "or the clergy would bloody soon be on the dole."

"Davy," said his mother, shocked.

Davy bent his square head over his plate, smiling to himself. Peter ate carefully, cutting his bread daintily on the side plate, the polite way. No banana-stroke now, teeth sinking deliciously into yielding bread, leaving a gaping semicircle in the piece. A clerical student could no more do that than he could rob orchards. Still, there were some fellows that knew how to sport themselves when on holidays. Swimming at Bundoran, playing Gaelic football with every parish team from Antrim to Kerry. His mother saw things with a splendid simplicity. Vocation to the priesthood meant to her a voice calling clearly, like a friend speaking casually over a green hedge. She could not understand the doubt, the revulsion, the resolution that was half remorse, the leap into darkness, the startled steadying of feet on unfamiliar ground. For her the voice called and man followed. God needed good priests. He knew His chosen ones.

"Come out and see the town," said Davy.

Devlin Street hadn't changed. The same small huckster's shop standing apart and separate. Facing it a block of grey houses, silent, with half-drawn blinds. All Protestants that lived there; their houses had a solemn, fur-capped Calvinistic appearance. The shoemaker's, the forge, the poultry-dealer's yard, the block of white shabby houses. All Catholics. When Peter was a lad a fire had gutted one of those houses. The awkward, excited crowd, the man with the fire-extinguisher that wouldn't work; the man cursing and hammering the extinguisher on the ground, the flames crackling.

They carried out a burnt woman, and laid her on a door torn off its hinges until the ambulance came. Peter could see her. Big and fat, covered with a dark rug. She moved a white naked arm, and cried with pain. Memories. Memories. Every inch of the street, every doorway had its meaning. The pub at the corner of Devlin Street. The beggar woman with the young, beautiful face and the baby at her breast. His mother had pitied her, given her pennies. Then playing gangs with Jerry Coyle in the yard behind the pub. He had seen her bargain with two drunken cattle-drovers. The baby slept on a heap of straw.

The sunlight of innocence passed that way. A lad at a day-school, with a freedom that lads closed in boarding-schools lacked, was in the way of gaining knowledge, good and evil. Those were the anxious years when knowledge came by insinuation, innuendo, the sly story half-understood, the reference at the street-corner to some shabby, ill-walked girl. His native town had marked him during those years. He looked back through them as through a tunnel to the faint light, the lost light. With man's years knowledge was rounded and complete, pleasure was related to its purpose, understood, controlled. But the knowledge gained in the tunnel, in secrecy, left its mark.

In Dublin Street Davy said:

"You're damned sociable."

"Sorry, I was thinking."

"Thinking: About what? Your morning meditation?"

"About the way we grew up here. When we were lads."

"Aren't you satisfied with the rearing you got?

Wasn't it good enough?"

"Too good. We were told about all the good things, not about the bad."

"That's a rare remark from a clerical student. Do you feel the loss now?"

"I lost no knowledge. When you played football and went fishing I completed my education. But it was all in a left-handed way. From the army reservists at the street corner.

"Wasn't that good enough? You didn't want your mother to tell you the sort of a girl Jinny Kane was."

"I saw Jinny Kane on the railway bank one Sunday evening. Then I knew."

"You'd 'a' been better employed fishing. Anyway, you'll find mortal sin anywhere. As a lad grows up gathering sense, he'll learn the difference between good and bad, between a woman like Jinny Kane and Rita Keenan."

"You're preaching now, Davy. Poor Jinny may have been weak or unfortunate. But bad? Who knows?"

"Open your eyes. You're the rarest bloody clerical student I've ever heard. Would you come out with the like o' that from the pulpit?"

"There was Magdalen."

"Black's black and white's white."

Davy snapped a match, sucked a cigarette, ending the argument. Outside the Pantheon Cinema men and women from the country waited on the bus, crowding the sidewalk: shopkeepers from small towns, prosperous farmers from the valleys, lean, gnarled, mountainy men, women with laden baskets. They zigzagged through the crowd, stepping over parcels and baskets, gently pushing and excusing themselves, colliding with two young men who stood chatting. One of the two turned, recognised the brothers, greeted them.

"Welcome home, Peter."

"Thanks, boys. You look well, Jim Carson." Jim Carson laughed, fingered the gold ring in the lapel of his coat, spoke in Irish to Davy.

"I've got my own school now, Peter. A good manager and the best parochial hall in Ireland."

"Ready to marry any day," said Peter.

"As soon as you're ready to do the job."

Carson steadied his heavy black-rimmed spectacles with his thumb and forefinger, stroked his broad, good-natured chin. He said:

"I'd marry if I could get a woman I wanted to marry. Arthur Williams here could spare me half a dozen."

They walked on together, Peter in the centre where Carson had noisily placed him as a mark of honour to the Church. Noisy talk and noisy jokes, carefully toned down because Peter was now a clerical student. He wouldn't have minded in the old days, thought Carson. But the black coat made a difference, cut a fellow off, separated him. Not so much the black cloth as what it stood for: the softness of vestments, the vague odour peculiar to the sacristy, the hands lifted in sacrifice, in forgiveness, the power to bind and loose.

The streets were filling; carts and cars from country places, cyclists pushing up the last slope to the centre of the town. Two green buses with clay-coloured, protective-coloured roofs, emptied cramped passengers on to the sidewalk. A string of dull military lorries went past; two gun-carriers on noisy caterpillar wheels. The four friends turned out of the main street, down a slope, under an archway into the market-yard. The sandy soil was bare, tramped naked of grass by generations of feet shuffling around the stalls of the buyers and sellers. Dealers in old clothes, pot-menders, patent medicines, opened their packs, waited for the market-day customers in from the country. In the shelter of the grey wall separating the market and the railway station, sellers of fruit and flowers polished red apples, laid out plants. In the corner near the river a herd of hobby-horses made their solemn circle, rising and falling, rising and falling. The tinny organ blared, warming up for the business of the day.

"Do you mind the time, Peter," said Carson, "we worked the slot-machines with the flattened tintops?"

Peter remembered: caps of lemonade bottles hammered the shape of pennies, the one that stuck, Carson hammering and shaking the machine, cursing schoolboy curses. The showman running after them, the race round and round the stalls and the caravans, the thin, grey woman at the caravan door calling for the police, the showman cursing when Carson shouldered him into a fruit stall—not schoolboy curses.

"We grow respectable," said Carson. "I couldn't do it now. I'm a teacher. That was the evening we went up the railway line with the two wee girls from the Loreto Convent. The train came. The Belfast express. You remember?"

Two lassies in blue blazers and navy skirts running before the train. Two schoolboys shouting to them, for God's sake jump, down the banking. A red-headed, stout girl that Carson had thought the world of, made him years older when the poor child died in a Belfast sanatorium. A thin, dark girl now grown to a woman, dark and shapely still, but grown hard, maybe bitter; turning the head of Davy with foolish dreams.

He said quietly: "Let the dead past . . .".

"What odds,!" said Carson. "It's gone now, like something out of somebody else's life. Poor Mary. The way she ran that day you'd never think she would die of consumption.

The other two had walked over to a fruit stall, gesticulatlng in hot argument.

"It would be a strange thing," said Carson, "if Davy and Rita Keenan made a match of it."

"Strange?"

"She never forgets. One of those dark ones. The shrouded few."

"It would be hard for her to forget."

"What happened, Peter, to drive you away?"

"People wake up."

"A man wouldn't need to be asleep to fall in love with Rita Keenan."

The hobby-horses circled solemnly, a frightened child clinging to the neck of one of them, delighted and afraid. A train screamed into the station. Peter said: "I mean that I saw our ways were different. She had her life to live and I had mine. Anyway, we were only children."

"Well, I suppose when God calls a man . . . and you always were a nick better than the rest of us."

"Let the dead past . . ."

"I'm sorry, Peter. I shouldn't mention things like this to you now. That's all dead and gone."

They followed Davy and Williams past the flowers and the fruit: hothouse flowers, fruit wrinkled and lacking the moist plumpness of autumn. Past the railway station where people from the small towns went in crowds towards the market and the shops. Out of the town along a quiet street, the red metal of gasometers rising above a grey wall, the heavy smell of gas in the air, the dust of coal like fine sand under their shoes. The wintry sun shone on flat fields, the full flowing river, the humpy arch of an old bridge of grey stone. The King's bridge, as old as James and Derry, Lundy and Walker, impotent guns gaping over a new huddled city, a gallant story twisted into a mad legend, giving virulent force to ignorant hate. Dead and gone. Dead and gone. The soldiers that crossed here. The queer king that lost his crown. Each man an individual story, tragedy and comedy, love and hate melted down into one mad legend of Orange and Green. Dead and gone also the stout lassie who ran panting for the Belfast train. Dead and gone the dark girl whose beauty was a force hinted at, a spring straining for release. . . .

On the road beyond the bridge, between flat fields under naked giant trees she met them. A black spaniel ran at her heels, darting right and left to snuffle at the hedge roots, tearing at the dead leaves with quick paws. Hard walking had given colour to her face, had tumbled a curl of dark hair on her forehead. Carson said: "Rita, your looks improve every day." She bowed, mocking him. "Your looks don't, Jim. The cares of teaching have marked you."

"This," said Williams, "is like old times. When the boys at school used to sneak out to see the Loreto girls."

"Afraid of their life of Mother Christopher," said Carson.

"I remember the day," said Rita, "she found the letter you sent to Betty Carr."

"On behalf of another," said Carson. "He used to read Betty's letters to me under the desk during religious instruction. They were very literary. All about Barkis is willin'."

"Betty was willin'," said Williams.

They laughed together, turning backwards towards the town. Peter and Carson walking ahead, the girl between them.

"Come to see us before you go, Peter," she said.

"Would I be welcome?"

"The door is always open."

"Thanks, Rita. As soon as the fuss of Christmas is over."

"We'll be expecting you."

She said good-bye at a street corner. Peter and Davy walked home, up the hill, past the courthouse. Their father, in off delivery, looked up from his plate as they entered.

"Got a temporary job for you, Davy, sorting letters for the Christmas rush."

Halfway down the stairs Mary called: "Davy wouldn't sort a letter for the King."

"Under stress," said Davy, "I'll take his money. It's dirty money all the same."

"The letters should belong to the Irish republic," said Peter.

Davy grinned, pulling his chair close to the table.

"Couldn't they get an Orangeman for the job?" he said.

V

The Quinns went to the six o'clock Mass on Christmas morning. That was a family custom; father and mother, sons and daughter marching solidly through the chill darkness. Shadowy groups clumped down the street, going in the same direction, the neighbours from Devlin Street, country people coming in by the Kilragh Road, the Calvinistic houses sound asleep, lights glimmering from the windows of the other houses, firelight, lamplight, the red glow of Christmas candles, the loud bell swinging in the spire, thundering through the darkness. This year no lights and no bell, silence and darkness, all over the world the great shadow, men watchful along the frontiers that divided the nations of Europe, men running from red ruin, mothers clutching children and running in blind terror listening for the rasp of engines in the air.

The Quinns walked together to six o'clock Mass. The people crowded around the marble rails in the half-lighted church, packed into pews, knelt in the aisles. High in the shadows the choir sang *Gloria* and *Adeste*; the priest preached, war and peace, we must pray for peace, give us peace, Lord, in our days—*Da pacem nobis, Domine.* Burned homes, broken shrines, hordes of men shaking the earth, the roar of engines in the air.

Peter crushed his face in his hands, trying to pray. No peace without, no peace within. Peace is certainty, definite purpose, a known aim.

Davy sat up, tenderly rubbing one knee, seeing the priest in the pulpit, hearing his words. Davy's mind was far away. The German had them this time, the day Mitchel and Tone had sighed for, Ireland free, Ireland Gaelic, fools and the Fenian dead.

Mary passed her beads steadily through thin, clean fingers, praying with a definite purpose.

They ate breakfast by the light of a red Christmas candle that was fixed in a blue glass jug and held firm by twigs of berried holly. The spirit of peace loosened the old man's tongue, set him talking, remembering boyhood in a little village by the sea, coastguards, smugglers, the tribe of red-headed tinkers who made poteen, the landlord shot dead because he took one girl too many as a maid to the castle, good days and bad days, the drunken schoolmaster, the clerical student drowned when boating, the escaped lunatic walking one June day into the schoolhouse, evictions, the priest arrested for preaching against the landlords, the fishermen in flat boats stabbing the fluke when the tide rolled in over the sand of the estuary. Every Christmas then was a white Christmas, snow seven feet deep in mountainy places.

Mrs. Quinn let the blind up with a snap. The candle burned pale in the morning light.

"Lies enough," she said.

"No lies," said the old man, slipping back into silence. Mary tied an apron around her waist.

"Davy, if Peter an' you went for a long walk, Ma and myself might get the turkey roasted."

"So we're not wanted."

"It's not you, Davy dear. It's the length of Peter's legs and the bigness of your feet. The house is small."

"Come on, Peter," Davy said. "She'll have your clothes ruined with sparking grease."

They left the town by the Kilragh road, past the red and white creamery, under the railway bridge. People who didn't rise so early were going to the ten o'clock Mass. The two brothers walked hard, up one hill and then another, the road under them stiff with frost, until the roofs of the town and the spires were below in the hollow, reflecting the wintry sun. White frost cracked and melted, loosening its grip on the stiffened grass, falling drip-drip from bare branches. The clean cut of the air stirred them like a rich drink, sent them walking on their toes, arms swinging.

"How long will it be now?" asked Davy.

"Three years."

"Then you'll be Father Peter, an' the boys will be lifting their caps to you."

"Yes."

"Are you content now?"

"I'm not discontented. Looking forward to that's like looking forward to eternal salvation. No matter how strong your faith is you can't imagine what the reality will be like."

"Like being in love with somebody."

"When you're in love you have a human contact like solid ground under your feet."

Davy considered. "Suppose now you were in love with someone. Really in love. The someone likes you well enough . . . she's glad to see you. But all the time something escapes you, the soul, like an eel wriggling out of your fingers.'"

"That's not a new problem. The soul of the other person always will escape us."

Davy kicked a stone loose from the grip of the frost, flung it over the hedge at a gaunt crow, grizzled with frost, wings weary with winter and the lack of sun.

"I suppose you're right," he said. "Now if people only told us what was in their minds."

He walked on, giving up the problem, puzzled by the twisted ways of the heart, falling back on the things he understood, a straight road to walk on, direct, intelligible actions of the body. They turned the spur of the hill, passed a cottage, went under a long avenue of bare trees to the shore of a lake. No wind moved the dark water held like a polished mirror in a hollow of the hills. A few desolate birds stood uneasily on the ice that fringed the reedy shore, moved picking in the hard shore grass.

"Pete and Jacob are still there," Peter said. He pointed across the water to the far shore where a small house stood, behind it a round, wooded hill.

Davy said: "Smoke from the chimney. They're doing the turkey."

"We'll go across to see them."

"Around that lane? You'd be muck to the two ears."

"Not in the frost. Come on, Davy. You're not afraid of mud."

Davy followed him over a small bridge, through a gateway, on a rutted cart-pass leading away from the road along the shore. On their left a rough heathery hill went up steeply, shadowing the lake, shutting out the little heat of the sun. He frowned at the shoulders of Peter's black coat, following with hesitation.

"Come on, slowcoach. You're not afraid of Pete and Jacob."

"They're maybe in bed."

"They were at Mass."

"Not they. They're too old to get out in the morning."

"Too old! Isn't Pete still courting?"

"Has been for the last sixty years. But the girl died last year. She was eighty, unmarried and a virgin. Pete's eighty-five."

"That's constancy for you."

"It's a laughing-stock. An' Pete rotten with money. Living in dirt an' walking the same lassie for sixty years."

"It's a tragedy. Even if it was their own fault."

"The country's filled with their like. Not quite so bad, maybe. Selfishness. It's a disease. Afraid of the responsibility of a wife. Afraid of children never born."

Peter went forward, thoughtfully picking his steps. When his mother was a baby Pete was a young man beginning to court. Pete's mother was a sonsy woman, generous, capable, a great housekeeper, a great baker and buttermaker. Dealers came from six or seven little towns to bargain for that butter, the rich creamy cleanliness of it. Peter's mother remembered meals eaten in that house on a table scrubbed bone-white, strong tea, fragrant hot bread with golden butter melting into it. Then the old woman died leaving two sons; and the life went out of the house. Jacob walked the fields, his thin shoulders bent. Pete tramped once a week to the house of his woman, slaved on the land, hoarded every penny, watched the house slipping back into the grass and mud. . . .

The house faced the lake where the lane ended. They picked their steps over the muddy street to the door. Davy cursed, wiping his shoes clean on the grass growing around the walls.

"What did I tell you? Muck that no frost could harden. The street wasn't cleaned since Pete fell in love."

He rattled the door. The thaw dripped on them from the dirty thatch. A few wild birds squabbled and fluttered at the edge of the lake, rose, flapped through the cold air over the black barn to the side of the house, over the bare trees. Within, feet shuffled, a chain rattled.

The door creaked open.

"Hello, Jacob," said Peter.

He blinked at them out of the smoky half-light. Strong smelling turf smoke rolled out to the frost. A thin face, wrinkled brown skin drawn tightly over bone, bald-headed, eyes dull. Behind him Pete spoke.

"Who is it?"

"Davy Quinn."

Pete came to the door, startling in his rank health, the whiteness of his hair over a face reddened with sun in the fields and smoke at the hearth.

"Jacob, you cod, open the door to the lads. You too, Peter. God, boy, it's years since I've seen you. An' the mark of the oil nearly on you."

The floor had once been flagged, grey flagstones polished with cleanliness, lost now under years of tramping muddy feet. Light struggled in through one tiny window, showing the bare dresser, the heaped bags of meal, flour, cattle-food; around the hearth and the outshot bed the red glow of burning turf. Peter entered cautiously, regretting the impulse that had brought him to the house, wondering what talk of Christmas he could make to two old men — one broken in body and wandering in mind, the other almost evil in the red flame of health denying old age. They loved wretchedness as normal men loved light and cleanliness. Davy was before him, talking to two men who sat by the hearth.

"I didn't bring him," said Davy.

A voice said : "Provided nobody saw you."

Davy said: "Safe enough."

Jacob closed the door, hooked a rusty chain to a nail, pushed home a creaking bolt. One of the men by the fire stood up.

"Happy Christmas, Peter," he said.

"Jim Carson. I didn't expect to find you here."

"Why not, Peter? Jacob an' myself are like that an' that." He crossed two fingers. "We do the town together every Saturday night. Don't we, Jacob?"

Jacob laughed, slavering, mumbling. He shuffled up from the door, heavy, laceless boots on his feet, commenced tidying a greasy raincoat that acted as tablecloth.

"You know Dick Slevin," said Carson.

The other man didn't move from his seat. He stretched out a hand and Peter advanced, eyeing the dark, narrow face, smooth, oily hair, the nervous, black, pin-prick eyes.

"Davy told me you were in England."

Slevin squinted sideways into the fire, giggled knowingly.

"I was."

"Did you like the civil service?"

"Fair enough. But the lads were being called up."

"Did you quit then?"

"They sent me. Deported. A bomb went off in our neighbourhood. Blew the side wall out of a building. They were suspicious."

"Were you in gaol?"

"God, no. Gentlemanly deportment or deportation. Deportment is what the nuns give the girls prizes for. The English cops are too polite to be true. Not like these Orange . . ."

He stopped, giggled again sideways into the fire.

"Saving your presence, Peter," he said. "My feelings run away with me."

"Dick's wanted here," Carson explained. "He's on the run."

"I wouldn't mind," said Slevin, "if they had anything against me. Raiding the house three nights a week. Got a job in the canteen at the barracks an' they were on my heels. The bloody Lodge does it, passing concocted stories to the cops. Somebody does it."

He spat into the hot ashes, giggled again. Peter, watching the thin, white fingers twine and retwine, knew the giggle for the battle-cry of an angered animal.

"Sit down, Peter," said Davy.

"My chair," said Carson. "It's a good while since the Church had a representative in this house. Not since the gentleman goat made an attack on the missionary father that came to persuade Pete to go to his duties."

Pete, Carson and Davy sat on the edge of the bed, the old man in the centre, grotesque with his flowing white hair, his flaming red face. Jacob stood in the background, picking with an unclean finger in his gapped teeth, shifting feet nervously, watching a closed pot-oven that dangled from the crane over the fire. The smell of something cooking, heavy and greasy, troubled Peter's nose. Across the red glowing circle he watched Slevin, the twining fingers, the tiny black eyes, the neat, tough body.

Pete said: "We're not gospel-greedy. But we don't owe a red penny to saint or sinner."

He bellowed startlingly incongruous laughter. Carson poked him in the ribs.

"Owe," he said. "You old rascal, an' you rotten with money. Tell me, Pete, what, portion of your will goes to the starving schoolmaster?"

Pete leaned forward, serious all of a sudden, pointing with a great finger over Slevin's neat shoulder. Peter's imagination saw Slevin against a background of flame and snow.

"Half my money goes to the Church to educate poor boys for the missions. It's a great work. An' half to the cause.

He concentrated his attention on Peter. "I held a gun too, you know. Your father was the man taught me how to use it."

"You didn't kill many men, did you?" joked Carson.

"The guns weren't so good then. But we drilled. We roasted the police out of a barracks. An' we blew up a bridge. Blew it sky-high."

Slevin giggled, shifting uneasily in his seat. Jacob shuffled his way to the fire, bent over the pot-oven, raised the lid. The smell strengthened. Peter saw suddenly a long refectory, laundered cloths, clean white cups, shining knives. He stood up.

"The day's passing, Davy."

"I'll be back into the town with you," said Carson.

"Come back soon," said Pete. "You too, Peter, to give us your blessing."

Jacob closed the door behind them, the chain rattled, the bolt snapped home. Davy and Carson led the way down the lane between the lake and the heathery hill. Peter followed: seeing the dark, dirty kitchen; the neat man by the fire, giggling, spitting into the hot ashes; the red health of Pete, the shambling good nature of Jacob. Walking with the same woman for sixty years, growing old, the blossom withering without fruit, the red blossom. The beauty of it sent young men walking alone, giving voice and form from their imaginations to something seen in solitude. Pete must have loved once, hoped for something, gone eagerly to learn fighting. Then the wall of selfishness was raised and the end was in dark rooms, unclean rooms, food smelling of grease.

Carson was saying: "It's a poor way to spend Christmas."

"Better than gaol," said Davy. "He's free. Isn't he?"

VI

She lived in Main Street. On Boxing Day Peter called to see her. The street before the shop was crowded, red-coated men on horses, red-coated women, men and women with ordinary dull clothes, a noisy pack of hounds, listless spectators. Katie, the maid, opened the door, the hall-door opening into a long passage separated from the shop by a thin partition. He followed Katie's corseted stiffness up the stairs into the living-room. Rita sat in a low chair near the window, bending forward slightly to look into the street.

"Katie," she said, "tell Daddy that Peter is here. Sit down, Peter."

He sat near the fire, watching the room reflected in the heavy overmantel: the solid, well-cushioned chairs fashionable forty years ago; the ornate grapes-and-flowers sideboard; the period portraits, figures in a dark centre against a white, empty background, women in great skirts; whiskered, stiff-collared men.

"Not interested in the harriers, Peter?"

"Not much."

"Wouldn't blame you."

She moved from the window, depositing the fruit-dish on a tiny inlaid table, came to sit facing him across the glow of the fire. She went on talking, hastily.

"The harrier people are a class. Or the remnants of a class. They've degenerated so much that the foxes left the country. If they rise a few hares now they consider their luck's in. They ride round fields too, looking for the gate."

Peter smiled: He said: "Poor Somerville and Ross."

"Of course," she said, "this never was a great country for hunting. The farmers must have thought too much of their land. The Presbyterians were great men for barbed wire."

Down in the street a horn blared. The dogs bayed. She said: "John Peel, how are you!"

He watched her pale face taking a blush of heat from the glow of the fire. Loosened hair fell down dark on the shoulders of a white blouse. A dark skirt curved with her slim muscular body. She crossed her ankles, lazily stretching towards the heat, and for a moment he was conscious of something familiar displayed by the discarding of that self-protective hardness. He caught his breath, troubled, perplexed. The door opened and her father came into the room. A big, genial man in his late fifties. Fair hair had turned grey and thinned, leaving an abnormally wide expanse of forehead above a round, healthy face. There was loose good-nature in the cut of his great limbs. The compactness of body, the thrusting force of the spirit in his daughter came obviously from the dead mother. He swung forward a great hand.

"Welcome, Mister Quinn. And how did you get over Christmas?"

"Very well indeed, Mr. Keenan."

"Quiet, I suppose."

"That's a blessing nowadays."

"Do you think will Hitler beat them?"

"Maybe."

The big man went silent, staring into the fire, thinking of the weekly pension that came to him as a retired sergeant of the old Irish constabulary. The war would hit the cloth trade. Every shilling counted.

He said: "I hope to God not."

Rita, rising, passed round the fruit-dish. They munched, talking little.

Rita said: "You'll eat something, Peter?"

"Not after a Christmas dinner."

"You can have the leavings of ours. We live on scraps for the week after Christmas."

"This war is bad," said her father. "Now, in the last war there was money to be made. Carneys made it in sawmills, Dohertys made it at coachbuilding and at the groceries. They own the town now."

"That money won't pass the third generation," said the girl. "Look at Alec Carney drinking himself into paralysis."

"But this war isn't the same. No money to be made except at smuggling. Decent men ruined that never knew a day's idleness."

"It'll end sometime," Peter said.

"You're young, Mister Quinn. You haven't lived to see two wars. I have. When the last war was on I talked the way you talk now. Then we lived through the troubled times: shooting and burning, the riots in Belfast, feared of our lives, not knowing under God which side was the worst."

Rita chanted: "A policeman's lot."

"Then things settled an' we made our homes. We thought peace would last for ever."

In the street again the horn blared and the hounds bayed. They heard the clatter of moving hooves, the shuffle of feet. She walked to the window.

"There's Carter the milkman. He rides with the hunt now. They say his horse stops at every door when they ride through the town."

"Where's your brother?"

"Jack's down in the street watching the hunt. He left here to buy some new dance music in Jacksons, but the crowd held him."

"You still run the school?"

"They have me deaf," said the father. "An' dead for want of sleep. Two nights a week blowing music and teaching the town how to dance."

"It pays. Somebody else would do it if we didn't. Keenan's school of ballroom dancing. We teach Irish dancing now too. You should see the hall since we fixed it up. Painted in blue and gold."

"I'd love to."

She turned from the window, looked at the clock.

"We'd have time before dinner to look at it."

"I'm not hungry."

"Still, you'll eat something with us. For old time's sake."

She was suddenly smiling, almost blushing, her eyes alive and bright, the hardness melting and vanishing. He watched her, feeling some powerful attraction, some longing, then reacting into alarm at his own unspoken accordance with her mood, her whims.

From the hallway at the bottom of the stairs a side-door opened on a cobbled yard. He followed her across the cobbles to the green door of the dancing-hall, set into a wall of whitewashed brick. There was a cold emptiness in the place; two grates with fires set, the dead white wood and black flameless coal intensifying the cold. Coloured-paper hangings drooped dead and lifeless from the roof, ringed the four windows that from their higher level overlooked walls and back gardens, the slow river fringed with ice, the long bridge of red metal.

"We have a dance to-night. You should come, Peter."

She went up the steps to the platform used by the dance band. On a table she fingered at and opened a small portable gramophone.

"Wouldn't suit my cloth, Rita."

"You could look on. You needn't dance."

"Looking on isn't much fun."

"Do you want fun?"

Her eyes and mouth were laughing, but in her voice there was an echo of mockery, of malice. He looked through a window over the walls and gardens, the river, the red bridge. The mockery maddened him, showed him how easily he could end it, showed him also that it would never end unless he said certain words: a sentence, a phrase, and mockery would end leaving only laughter in the eyes, rich laughter on the mouth. He couldn't say the words. They would end a vision, seen dimly by himself, distinctly by his mother. No mockery with her, only patience, conviction, endless hope.

The needle scraped on a worn record, a band played scrapily, male voices sang, a ball-bearing rattled in each voice: "We're going to hang out our washing on the Siegfried line." She said: "Davy wouldn't like it. It's a new one. You can quick-step to it."

Davy. The name was reality, rock-bottom. He came away from the window, from the unreal dreams, the quicksands, the treachery of the twisting current that pulled and pulled. He said suddenly: "Put that thing off, Rita. I don't want to dance."

She laughed. "Nobody asked you."

The record played. She came slowly down the steps from the platform and stood by his side, her hand on his shoulder, lightly at first, then the fingers gripped and held as he made to move away.

"You don't need to," she said. "Even for you a friend is a friend. You needn't be on the defensive."

She ran up to the platform. Ceasing to think, he watched the swing of her dark hair against the thin silk of the white blouse, the dark skirt shaping itself to the moving of her limbs. She changed the record. The room filled with a splendid waltz-tune, music with a civilisation behind it, no cheap ragtime, no music- hall. Her body, the white and the black, the pale, serious face softening into laughter, moved with the music. They danced. The white silk was thin under his hand. Her fingers gripped his, her eyes shining. She said breathlessly : "You haven't forgotten how." There was no answer he could make. The music and movement went into his blood. The music, the dance, the dancers melted into unity. Through the window, as they whirled, he saw the river and the long, red bridge. Then the music stopped. The needle grated. He sat down on the steps while she lifted the needle off the record.

"Rita, don't play it again."

"Why, Peter?"

"I don't want to dance. That's why. I'm tired."

She came and sat down with him on the steps, a little above him. Eyes fixed on the ground he saw vaguely the dark skirt covering her knees. "Poor Peter," she said, "You work too hard." Her hand stroked his shoulder. He gripped it, pressed it quietly to his lips, felt her in his arms, is if another man had done a wrong thing and he, Peter Quinn, watched from a prudent, holy distance. She covered her face, leaning against him. He looked down on her dark hair, on the black cloth that covered his own arm encircling the white blouse. His own arm. The thought pressed in on him, filling his mind, crushing him into numbness. Horror at his own weakness sickened him, the yielding to an impulse that brought down in ruin the careful building of four years, discipline, order, resolution, prayer. Was it inherited, in the blood, like Davy's patriotism, in the blood of all men? She raised her head again and he pushed her from him, walking to the window, gripping the painted sill. Over the red bridge the hunt straggled, deserted of foxes, red coats and hungry hounds, riding round fields looking for convenient gates.

"That was terrible," he said.

She laughed, hiding her fright, shaking her head in a negative that filled him at once with anger and pity, repelling him and attracting him. There was a strange understanding between them, going back to their schooldays, to the long sunny afternoons, pigeons fluttering over the old irregular roofs of the town. Wherever they met in time to come they would be allies, in secret alliance, held together by memories of words and actions, by some community of spirit. He hardened himself.

"It was sinful," he said.

She repeated: "Sinful."

"I know it was my fault, Rita. I am what I am. Should have known better. Anything that was between us years ago. All dead now. There's no use in digging up the old skeleton again."

She stood up, carefully smoothing the dark skirt.

"Why don't you call me names?" she said. "Say I tempted you. Say I'm the occasion of sin."

"You didn't."

Her voice thinned into anger: "But I did. I wanted you to kiss me. Because I loved you. For years. Even before you went away to be a priest."

"We were too young."

"I wasn't. I was old enough to know my mind. I haven't changed. You took yourself away from me."

"God took me."

"What had God to do with it? Your own impulse. And deep down in you, you wanted to please your mother, because she was good, a good woman, a good mother."

"Stop, Rita."

"You know it's true. I nearly hate you for taking the blame on yourself, for being too deliberately good to see that I led you on."

"Rita, have sense. You're not that sort."

"What sort? We're all that sort. But some are afraid and some wouldn't for shame. I'm not afraid. I'm not ashamed. I love you so much I know you better than you know yourself. I know you're out of place where you are. You can't stand back a bit and look at yourself. You're not like the men who make priests, real priests. You're quiet and you read. But that isn't enough. Inside you're different. Maybe it's pride. You're not humble enough to live only with God. You want somebody else to teach you to laugh at yourself. You must find out the poor, laughable way men and women love each other."

"Stop, Rita."

"I love you," she said. "I love you."

"You're raving. You don't know what you're saying."

"Your brother should have been the priest. He's not clever and he's as loud as a saxophone. But there's no pride in him."

He crossed the room towards the door.

"Are you going, Peter?"

She was sitting weakly on the steps, the anger drained out of her, leaving her frail and crumpled, her white face, white and pitiful, hidden in her hands. At the door he turned and looked at her. He said:

"It's the best thing to do."

"You won't wait for dinner?"

"I'm not hungry."

"Daddy will be surprised"

"Tell him I was in a hurry. I've a lot of calls to make."

"Will we see you again, Peter?"

"Better not, Rita."

The tears on her face horrified him. He gripped the door, holding himself where he stood.

"I'm sorry, Peter," she said. "I'm sorry."

"My fault," he said. He opened the door.

"No," she said. "You're proud and silly. But you're not bad. I'm bad. But I'm not as silly as you are."

There was nothing he could say. He fumbled with the knob of the door, mumbled good-bye.

"Good-bye, Peter. Shall I go to the door?"

"No," he said. "I know the way."

He closed the door behind him, crossed the yard, through the hallway out to the street. The day had darkened. A cold Christmas wind dropped on the pavements the first wet crystals of the coming rain. The red hunters would get wet, forsaken of the foxes, following hares through conveniently opened gates.

2

Davy

I got a few weeks' work, right enough, out of the Christmas rush in the post office. Tons and tons of letters, white, brown and coloured, and me standing there in the sorting-office flicking them into their pigeon-holes. But, Heavens above, it isn't the sort of work I like. Too enclosed. No fresh air to talk about. Letters, parcels, dirty bags, stamps. I was glad when it was over and Peter back safe and sound in his college. He's the best in the wide world but he depresses me. So prudent and discreet. Then all of a sudden he comes out with something would make the hair stand on the head of an experienced corner-boy. That's the result of reading too much. Anyway, he went back to his job and I went back to mine at the plumbing of the new huts for the military, using the blow-lamp, leading roofs, bending copper pipes, doing work that helped me to conquer the twisted vexation of things. And it leaves me free to do what I damned well like with my spare time. A post-office worker would have to stop attending Gaelic classes with lads that keep one foot over the threshold of Belfast gaol.

God knows if it wasn't for the Gaelic classes, the light and the cheery company, a fellow would go mad in this town. We're in the war and we're not in it, neither fish nor flesh. We've got the blackout and rations. The streets are filled with soldiers. No honest enthusiasm anywhere. The Orangemen want their jobs and their domination. I want my job. I have to live. I help to build huts to house British soldiers, the army of occupation. Then I go home, take off my dungarees, listen to the German radio and believe every word of it. God, what a life!

At the class we talk in Irish, good Irish some of us, bad Irish others. We sit around the fire looking into the flames, talking about the Rosses, the grey Rosses. The coast is grey rock, sandhills here and there, rough headlands, beaches of red or white sand, and the green water tossing and turning all the time, changing colour like silk. Out beyond the islands is the great ocean and the next parish, they say, is Brooklyn. God send the summer, and maybe if I got a week's holidays I'd cycle across there, away beyond Errigal and Muckish mountains. The fields are tiny and the stone ditches as high as the houses. The people are friendly. The doors are open to strangers, low chairs ready at the red hearth. Old Mickey's Paddy bends over his stick, chewing and spitting, telling old tales that are a damned sight better than the talkies. The sun is hot on the rocks. Hudie's boat is crossing the water to the white strand. Peace and freedom and no soldiers. The war washes past under the rough ocean. Sometimes a piece of driftwood or a dead body, washed in to be buried in peace, comes up out of the sea

But here, Heaven help us, in this town we make the best of it with classes and parties and dances. Rita does take an interest in the dancing although she isn't so hot when it comes down to learning the language. Some people are funny that way. Slevin now is a fair example. That man actually did do something for his country. He got his walking-papers out of England and, from what I hear, he was lucky he didn't go into clink for five or ten years. The police here persecuted him, sent him on the run, left him with no home. But would he learn Irish? Not a chance. I gave him the books, but he handed then back to me and laughed like a jacksnipe. God, that laugh of his gives me the creeps. He said to me, Davy, says he, my love for Ireland is purely negative. Just so. Purely negative.

Maybe Rita's like that. Anyway, her love of country stops when the dancing stops. She's a rare one. Odd in her own way, although I grant you she has improved since Peter went back after Christmas. Was there ever any truth in the things Carson used to say about herself and Peter? It puzzles me. You never know with a fellow like Peter or with a girl like Rita. Deep as the ocean both of them. But he's out of the running now. Praise God.

II

She said she'd go up to the *céilidhe* in the big hall at Malltown, so

Carson and Arty Williams and myself hired Donnegan's hackney-car. It took us out of the town for a while. It killed Sunday, the deadest day in the whole dead week. Mass and breakfast and sitting around until dinner. Dinner and sitting around until tea. Tea, and watching Jack Carney smiling at Mary and Mary smiling back at Jack Carney, and Da and Ma smiling at each other with the sheer bloody content of it all. Ma's pleased and well she might. Jack's a good catch, a decent fellow and decent people and a good, steady job. Besides, he's sunk to the scalp in love with Mary. She's worth it too, even if her brother does say so. She looks good with the light shining through the long red hair. She's as honest as the day is long. Never told a lie in her life. It must be powerful to be in love with a girl like Mary and she in love with you. You know where you are. But the dark, quiet ones, God help us.

Well, we dodged Sunday. Jack and Mary wouldn't come, so we left them smiling at each other. We drove up over the mountain road, through dark flat bog with wee lakes shining in the heather. The big hall was crowded and the people dancing mad. They hammered away until midnight. Carson ran the show. He teaches in Malltown school. He came to Rita and myself when we were having our supper with Arty Williams and a teacher-girl from Strabane. His face was as long as a wet week.

Rita said: "Jim, did the doorman run away with the money?"

Williams said: "Somebody dead belonging to you?"

Carson took me by the sleeve and whispered in my ear that he wanted me for a minute. We went out of the refreshment-room, along the gravelled path by the side of the hall, through the gate, down the road under the trees to the schoolhouse.

I said: "What's up?"

He led me to a wee cloakroom at one end of the school. A lamp was burning there and the blackout blind tight on the one window. Slevin was sitting on a chair, washing his face in a basin of water that was red with blood. The clothes on his back were wet with muck. I said: "God above, what happened you?" I hadn't seen him since Christmas. He looked up at me and laughed, cleaning the blood from his face with a wet cloth. There was a soft red cut below his right ear.

"Hello, Davy," he said. "How's the' heart?"

He laughed again, squinting sideways into the basin.

"What happened you, Dick?"

"Jim'll tell you. I'm too busy. And Jim, could you ever change the water in the basin? You could send this as a blood-donation to the R.A.F."

Carson refilled the basin. I sat down and looked at Slevin. He squeezed the crimson out of the cloth, dipped it in clean water and began again.

Carson said : "He says he was cycling to a hide-out in the neighbourhood and had a spill."

I looked at the soft red cut. "Hell of a gash to get with a spill off a bike."

Slevin said: "It was a bad spill."

"Why don't you tell us the truth, Dick?" I said. "You know we're with you."

He dropped the cloth splashing into the water. His thin face turned towards me, not smiling the blood oozing out from the half-closed cut. "With me?" he said. "There's nobody with me." Then he laughed again and picked up the cloth. "Sorry, Davy. No offence. But what you don't know doesn't do you any harm. Would you give me a lift back to the town? I'm going back to the palatial residence of Pete and Jacob. The nearer the police the farther from gaol."

I thought for a while. Rita would be with us. It wouldn't be right to get her mixed up in any trouble. God alone knew what capers Slevin had been up to.

"Pete's dead," I said.

"God rest him," said Slevin. "True love unrequited and wild, unstinted generosity were the death of him. Still, he wasn't a bad old codger. Gave me the shelter of a roof when I couldn't find one anywhere else. Jacob will be lonely without him. He'll be glad of my company.

"There's room in the car," I said. "Jim's not coming back. He has to be at his desk here in the morning."

"Good for Jim," he said. "After the British Constitution the world's next most respectable thing is an Irish schoolmaster."

He laughed sideways, squeezing pink water from the cloth. I had a sudden feeling about him, that he was dangerous like barbed wire. Still, he had done something and suffered something.

Rita sat in the back of the car between myself and Slevin. His face was plastered with adhesive tape and he wore a clean suit that Carson had given him. Arty Williams sat in front with the driver. I wrapped the rug around her knees, cuddling her into it the way a mother would cuddle a child. She was very quiet and pale in the face, frightened maybe at Slevin's plastered jaw. She knew, the whole flaming town knew, that the man was on the run. A very white moon came up behind the mountains, shining down on the lakes in the flat bog. The car went on down towards the valley, the humming of the engine sending us half-asleep. I could feel her head slipping down and down until it rested on my shoulder and her fine dark hair tickled my face. She seemed to be softening towards me, taking me for a real friend. God forgive me, I thought of Peter in his cold room, the same white moon shining on the slates above his head. I wish I could forget the jokes Carson used to make. Unfair to Peter and to Rita to take Jim Carson seriously. The fancies of a boy and a girl, that was all.

The car hummed on, down into the valley. Rita dozed, leaning on my shoulder, turning towards me in her sleep, her bosom rising and falling with firm, steady breathing. My heart nearly stopped altogether. Williams and the driver talked softly to each other. I closed my eyes. Once when the car bumped over a little bridge I came awake and saw the black back of Slevin's head outlined on the window in the light of the moon, the thin black head, one jaw swollen with the bulk of white tape, very bitter and lonely. She leaned her head on my shoulder and dozed.

Five miles from the town we were halted at a crossroads. A wall of damp sandbags blocked half the width of the road. The specials stood around with their rifles at the ready. A big policeman bent his head and shoulders down to us. He said : "I'll see your licence and your identity-cards." The driver handed out his licence and his own card. Rita came awake. The engine buzzed. I pressed her hand, blind with terror that she would scream when she saw the long automatic that Slevin nursed on his knees. The crazy lunatic. Might have had the whole shooting-match of us perforated like sieves. The specials stood with their rifles at the ready. One of them came forward trailing the butt of his gun. Arty handed out his card. The cop read it, bent down again, reached into the car to touch Arty's shoulder. "Arty Williams," he said, "I declare to me God." They shook hands. I watched the automatic melt into the darkness between Slevin's knees. My grip on her hand loosened. She said: "Davy, you crushed me." Arty was talking with the cop, God knows about what. My head buzzed like the engine and I wanted to vomit. We drove past the barrier and the specials and their rifles, and on down the road. Arty said : "It's hellish funny the way you meet people. When we lived in Belfast and I was a kid I went to school with that fellow. He's in Malltown now."

"The world's a small place," said the driver.

"Lucky for us," said Slevin, and he laughed.

I thought: "Arty, you came damn near to losing a school-chum."

Rita snuggled down on the seat beside me, resting her head on my shoulder, taking me for a real friend. We drove into the town. The dawn was coming up grey and red, behind the church spire. At one corner we were halted for half an hour while soldiers tramped past, hundreds and hundreds of them carrying rifle and kit, tramping towards the station.

"For France," said the driver.

They joked and whistled. They sang that they were going to hang out their washing on the Siegfried line.

"They'll never see it," said Slevin.

"Some day," I said, "that uniform will go never to return. We'll be free then."

"God help them," said Rita. "Irish and English and Welsh, they've got mothers and sisters and girls maybe."

Slevin laughed sideways at the street. The courthouse clock high above us chimed the hour.

The Malltown shooting was in the Belfast morning paper. Four cops and four specials had surrounded a derelict house to arrest a wanted man. He killed a cop and wounded a special. They enquired at hospitals and with doctors for news of a wounded man. The dead cop left a widow and four children.

III

Slevin gives me the creeps. Never since God made me was I afraid of anybody, but that man is deadly. He has done something and suffered something. I don't deny it. The police did keep him on the move when he lived at home, but the way he remembers it isn't human. I said to him: "Dick, Kerrigan's lorry is going down to Derry. You could cross the Border and head for West Donegal, Gweedore or the Rosses. I know men there who'd shelter you willingly. You'd be as safe as a baby in its mother's arms." He laughed at me. Go to Donegal? What for? Police or no police he'd stay where he'd been bred and born. Did I want him to take to learning Gaelic with hairy natives in the desolate, shelterless Rosses, the last, the coldest and the rainiest place that God made? I got angry and told him he could do worse. Then he refused to come to our drilling in a meadow near Jacob's place. Said he could use a gun before I was born. Then he whipped out the long Mauser and stood pointing it at his own shadow on the filthy wall of Jacob's hut. It struck me suddenly that he likes the whole thing, like a playactor in the part of his life, dramatising himself as the hunted man, the lone wolf. Maybe I was wrong and uncharitable. God help him, if he's caught now he swings. A wanted man. They put out a reward notice for him, five hundred cool quid, his description in thick black print. Poor Dick.

He used to keep himself clean, his suit brushed, his hair licked flat. Now maybe Jacob's housekeeping has affected him. He doesn't give a damn, lets his beard grow, sleeps in his clothes. Jacob shuffles up and down, bent almost double since Pete was put under the clay, smiling and talking to himself, trailing his feet and the loose bootlaces tripping him. Great company altogether for a man with a price on his head. Around the house and around the lake spring is coming, new buds on the hedges, new growth in the grass, a new blue colour on the water. But inside that house there's no spring, there never will be a spring. It gives me the creeps.

The Gaelic classes are a break, and Rita. I leave her home from the classes these nights. The streets weren't too safe and that gave me the excuse. Sometimes she's in the best of humour, laughing and talking, linking me, half-swinging from my arm, making jokes about the dark streets and the soldiers rattling past and the couples wedged in doorways. Then the next minute she's as silent as a graveyard, thinking to herself, saying, "Yes, Davy," and "No, Davy," as if what I said didn't mean anything to her, as distant as the man in the moon. She was that way one night about a week ago. I left her to the halldoor and she stood quiet as if she had forgotten all about me. I said good night and turned to go when she caught me suddenly by the arm, her lips tight together as if she had made up her mind about something. "No, don't go, Davy," she said. She led me through the hallway, across the yard to the room where she teaches the dancing. I said : "Your da will throw me out. At this hour of the night."

She switched on the light and said: "Davy, some times I think this place is haunted. You must help me to lay the ghost."

She went up to the gramophone and put on a waltz record. It sounded like thunder in the quiet night. "Do you mind?" she said. "It's a foreign dance." Then she gripped me and we waltzed around the room. After a Gaelic class too. When the record stopped we sat down on the wooden steps that led up to the stage. "You don't believe in ghosts, do you?" I asked.

She leaned over to me and kissed me. You could have knocked me down with a feather. I said to her: "Rita, I love you." She snuggled her head against my chest and said: "Poor Davy. I believe you. You're honest with yourself and everybody else. God help you." Then I asked her would she marry me. She cried a little, a tear or two, and said "Yes," and I kissed her until the room spun around and around.

I went home that night my step as light as a feather. She's a strange girl. But I love her. Herself and her ghosts.

3

Peter

I

WHEN I was eighteen years of age, kneeling at Benediction, the hush, the smell of incense, the lifted monstrance, I made the resolution. Or it made itself, somewhere inside my head. It had been there for a long time, solidifying, gathering strength, but I didn't know it until the priest lifted the monstrance, the people bowed their heads and were quiet. Then I knew I wanted to be a priest. A resolution made in the exultation of music and symbol and drifting grey clouds of incense is not to be trusted. It's hard to be certain when exactly I found that out. Maybe it was the day Dowdall came to me in the planting between the house and the lake. In under the tall bare trees I swung a mattock, tearing a stump that marred the flatness of the ground, disciplining my body, blistering my fingers. He came up from the lake, behind him and between the trees the gleam of wintry water.

"Brother Peter," he said, "let Austin have his swink to him reserved."

I liked him because he liked books. The phrase from Chaucer came naturally from his lips, a literary ex-bank clerk from Dublin, very British in his politics. He could never get accustomed to shaving in cold water, to the monastic discipline that denied him marmalade with his breakfast. He sat down on the scarred stump, crumbled between his fingers a fragment of the decaying wood, and said : "*Domine, Domine, quis sustinebit*? Lord, Lord, who can stick it?"

"Have, you got blues?"

"Yes."

He rubbed his forehead, a high, square forehead, pushing back his dark hair.

"They're terrible, aren't they?" he added. "Very tiresome. I want Dublin."

"Dublin?"

"You're country, Peter. You'd never understand."

"Country town," I said. "A country town with two cinemas, a laundry, a lunatic asylum, a hospital, a county court, fifty pubs."

"No difference," said Dowdall. "It's country. Genuine rural life. You've no theatre, no cafés open late at night, shining lights, pretty waitresses."

"You're in the wrong place for that here."

"That's what's wrong. I am in the wrong place. I've just found it out. I don't know why I came here. There was a reason, but I've lost sight of it, like a loss of memory, a blank, a darkness."

He buried his face suddenly in his hands.

"Being here is reality. I touch this wood, rotten wood. I see you, Peter Quinn, mattock in hand. The wood, you, the mattock, are real. But I don't know why I'm here looking on. I am looking on. I don't fit into the picture. You do. So do the others, except a few. You'll all be good priests, giving your lives for God, going to teach all nations. I'll go back to Dublin, pick up my life where I left it."

"What is it that you don't like ?"

"Little things," he said. "Laughable things. They don't count. It's the awful feeling of misdirection, of ploughing rocks."

"The depression that has no ascertainable cause. . . ."

". . . is straight from the devil. I know. The monk's disease. The noonday devil."

I tumbled the mattock on the grass, sat beside him on the stump.

"Tell me, Dowdall. What are the little things?"

"To begin with," he said, "there's getting up in the morning. Five thirty-five. Now, under Heaven, why at that hour? Morning prayers in the church. Morning meditation. Menial tasks to teach us humility. Cleaning up the bathroom. Washing the dishes. Being charitable to each other, deliberately charitable, even to men I'd love to kick. I like study, not regulated and controlled study. I like games and walks, not regulated games and controlled walks."

"Necessary training," I said. "You wouldn't have us dancing, dicing and drinking."

"It wouldn't do," said Dowdall. "I know that. I'm not overfond of wild dissipation myself. But I get homesick for the queerest things. Last night now, honest to God, I dreamt I was in the Tivoli, up in the top gallery with the gods. I smelt the smell of the stone stairs that go up to it, a stale, unclean smell. You go up and up. You think you're on the roof. Then you look down, feeling dizzy, on the lighted stage, like standing on one planet looking through space at another planet, other lives."

"A funny dream."

"A memory. Between sleeping and waking my head fills with them. One night it was a dance hall, crowded to the door. Me shuffling around with some nameless girl. A dream-vision. Trying to make her hear what I was saying above the noise of the band. Not great fun. Still, it was life without regulation. Another night it was the tennis club. A June evening in a railed square between Georgian houses. Then a hike. Frying sausages on the moor near Lough Bray. Or drinking in a cottage in Howth, looking through the window at the white lighthouse and the pointed rock jutting out into the sea like the world's end."

The pictures came up before my eyes. His eyes shone. He made sudden gestures, forgetting me.

I said: "You give that up. You get it all back, a hundredfold, pressed down and flowing over."

"Not me. I haven't given it up. It's in my heart, swelling and swelling, smothering me. Listen, Peter. Last spring I was weeding the bed of red flowers in front of the house. A man and a girl came out of the plantation. She was a redhead, wearing shorts, good knees. Holiday people that had lost their way. He kissed her. They didn't see me. It was awful."

I laughed. "Have sense. People do kiss each other. It's not even a misdemeanour."

"It wasn't their kiss. But I knew then I had either made a mistake when I came here or . . ."

He stood up. I knew that he wiped a tear from his face, red water pressed out by some pain at the core. I kept my eyes on the ground in pity and shame.

". . . or that I had lost my vocation. Don't know which. I'll never know. That's the trouble with people like me."

He walked away from me, going between the trees towards the

house. At recreation after supper he was cheerful, abominably cheerful, charitable to everyone. We knew next day that he had gone back to Dublin. Not knowing, never to know. It's like meeting yourself in some dark, lonely street, that seeing your own problem staring at you out of another man's eyes.

II

The bell rang and we rattled down to recreation. The long corridor filled with the rich darkness of late winter, alive and conscious of the coming spring. One red lamp burned before the statue of the Sacred Heart. Peterson knelt on the prie-dieu, his head in his hands, his feet getting in our way as we went past, sixty of us. We disturbed him. There was irony in that, for Peterson was one of the few who had a sort of right to be there. People like Peterson had owned that house, danced, dined, got drunk, sinned, were virtuous, rode off to hunt, left for the London season. They, the squires, fox-hunting landlords, had separate standards, different morals, distinct social values. Their very accent sounded Irish to the English and English to the Irish. Peterson had the intonation.

They had moved up and down that corridor, slept in the rooms, tossing uneasily or in hot, contented bliss. They passed, and the priests of a new people dined and slept and prayed in the same rooms. The ballroom was a chapel. Two rooms with the intervening partition removed made the refectory. A stone lion-and-unicorn still remained above the great Doric entrance. The government of a new liberated people tumbled the great wall circling the estate, built new homes on small farms, planted green acres of young trees, leaving the gardens and lawns to the priests and students. The classical century had left its traces. There was a stone grey-bearded Socrates behind a rhododendron clump. A very young student had once taken the statue as representing Saint Joseph. Diana, grey stone nose broken, looked across the weedy lake at Actaeon running from the hounds. The broken nose cut a sneer into her face. There was a Greek temple in a clump of trees. They used to carry the old lord there, to cool him off after his wine.

We, the new people, rattled down the corridor, Peterson, distracted, rose, mingled with us, followed us.

In the ambulacrum we walked and talked between the statue of Xavier and the statue of Saint Patrick. Our spiritual director came with a visitor, a tall, well-built clergyman, a German. We gathered around, interested. Every visitor was welcome, news, a contact with the outer world. He sat on a chair and talked, the words pushed out of him, long and rounded. He was an exile along with other members of his order, their house in Austria seized by polite local officials who were never responsible but who acted under orders from other men who were exceedingly polite but still were not responsible. He built a new home in an Irish midland village by a flat canal lined with thin poplars. The tailor in the village had fought opposite him in the trenches in the first world war, the valiant Dublin Fusiliers, the Connaught Rangers. He told stories of war. Our director, thin and grey and kindly, told funny stories about the 1916 rising. We laughed at our own little fight, were respectfully serious about his big fight.

Then the bell rang again. We said the Litany of the Saints in the chapel. We went to bed. The long cedar branches outside my window creaked in the wind. A lost people had planted them. Dead beauties sailing in great skirts had loved the cedars, the beauty of Lebanon. The face of the German priest was in my dream and behind him the lands of the earth living with armies, miles and miles from that house of prayer, from the creaking cedars. The world, the disturbed world, and poor Dowdall with no quiet in his soul going back to the world because it too was unquiet and in turmoil. Poor Dowdall.

III

To begin with, there was getting up in the morning. I didn't mind that. Shaving in cold water didn't annoy me. Marmalade had no particular attractions for me. Still, there was something that made me different from the men who persevered. At study in my room it was noticeable, a feeling of unreality, unfamiliarity, a sense that I wasn't at home. She said I was too proud to be a good priest. Only the humble could afford to escape the humiliating dependence of human love. But I could have classified *her*, put her into her category as a temptation, if only the other thing, the dark unrest, had not disturbed me. My bad angel, my good angel, one whispering into each ear when I bent like Faustus over my table.

Nostalgia for the little town, the ridged roofs, the fluttering doves, the sun slanting round tall spires, the circle of quiet blue hills behind Ballyclogher? Dowdall was sick, desiring Dublin. No, not in my case. The little town meant eyes slanting out of dark doorways, clacking tongues, no possibility of losing oneself in the swirl of a city. I would be the returned-empty. My people. My mother. If I had really considered her I would have stayed against my wish, even against the black knowledge of my own error. She lived for one thing, to watch the swing of my heavy vestments, my lifted hands. If I had really wished to make her happy I would have strangled my own conscience when it suggested to me that I was wrong. My conscience? The devil? I'll never know. That's the trouble with people like me. We never know.

The March wind was cutting the tears from our eyes. On the flat steps before the house I said good-bye to the Father Superior. A taxi waited, parked on the blue gravel. The engine hummed. A black cloud tumbled across the cold blue sky. The Father Superior said: "It'll rain."

I said: "On the just and the unjust."

He laughed, a quiet, grey-headed laugh. He held out his hand, gripped mine and said: "You'll be a good man, Peter, anywhere." God help us, I wanted to weep. I said: "I'll do my best, father."

"Even if our way of life didn't suit you, you'll find the world stands in need of good Christian men. The poor world."

I went down the steps, into the car, sat crumpled up between cases, my eyes closed. The engine hummed and hummed. The car scattered gravel at the avenue gate where the pitiful little village clustered, then bumped over the canal bridge. The poor world. The poor tormented, tumultuous world, stretched on the rack, nailed to the cross, the bleeding, the wounded, the speechless, the mangled dead, the broken homes. Her face came behind the lids of my eyes; crumpled and white, wet with tears.

The country was alive with spring, the warmth and force of it bursting into buds in the high hedges, making the road white, crisp, inviting. At least restraint was behind me, shackles I was never meant to wear. Had I only imagined them? Was I certain? All men were shackled in one way or another. The others would go on living the same life, feeling no restraint, quite happy, accomplishing and completing.

After Confession, Father O'Connor had said: "My child, you are not happy here." I felt very old, not a child. He leaned forward, his thin face, the smooth forehead, the scarce grey hair. He raised his hand in blessing and forgiveness. He said again: "My child, you are not happy here."

The train steamed up through the flat midlands, the slow canal, the lady poplars. Father O'Connor told the truth. His advice was good. It gave me certitude. No more hateful doubt.

A cold spring wind cleaned the streets of Dublin, twisted and tossed the Liffey water. I stood outside the cinema watching the crowds go up and down the pavement, hoping for Dowdall, not seeing him. My train went after three hours. He at least could lose himself in the city.

4

The Pit

I

HE came on the morning train and there was nobody at the station to meet him. There was no pride in his homecoming. The long, sunny platform was almost deserted. A soldier sat and smoked. A postman gathered slack, forlorn mail-bags. He dodged the postman's eye, gripped his two cases, made for the exit. Outside the station one hackney waited, the driver seated on the running-board, calmly chewing a blade of grass. The driver said : "I'll drive you home, Peter. There'll be no customers off this god-damned train. There never are."

"I wouldn't trouble you."

"No trouble at all. Get in. I'm going your way."

They drove off, around the corner by the hoarding, up the hill into the town. The driver said: "Isn't it bloody well awful?" Peter said it was. "The cool bloody nerve of him," said the driver. "Marching in like that an' chasing the Danes out in their shifts. Be God, they're not the sons of the men that fought at Clontarf or they'd put up a better show." Peter said "Yes." He had forgotten the war.

"They say he's making for Norway too. God help us all."

A line ran in Peter's head: "From Noroway, from Noroway, from Noroway over the foam." They drove past a squad of soldiers in shirt and trousers, marching irregularly, whistling a German military march, banging tin plates and enamelled mugs.

"Do you think, Peter, will it hit the banks?"

"God knows. Don't care myself. I've no money."

"I have a wee bit put by. Not much. A few pounds.

It worries me. You know, if anything was to happen. The weans.

The lassie's just started at the boarding-school. Mother Christopher says she's the quickest pupil ever entered the place.

They drove up Devlin Street, the huckster's shop, the white papist houses, the grey Calvinistic houses.

"You're home for the big day, Peter."

He said absently: "Big day." The driver laughed, pushing his cap back off his forehead, swivelling round in his seat as the car halted.

"Go on now, man. I'm booked to drive the bride. A lovely girl, "God bless her. Carney's a lucky man."

Peter went up the steps. He paused with his hand to the knocker watching the car go away down the street. Big day? It wasn't too late yet. He could go back to the station, take the first train to Dublin, find Dowdall, lose himself in the city. They were standing in their rooms now, quietly saying the Angelus. Then down to lunch in the cool, white refectory, green grass and young flowers outside the window, the spring breathing life into the great trees, into the vegetation on the lakeshore, where a damaged Diana sneered across flat water at a petrified Actaeon running from petrified hounds. The car went on down Devlin Street, turned the corner and vanished. Tomorrow it would drive the bride.

II

Mary was married in white. Her long, red hair tumbled down on her shoulders. Davy was groomsman, and Jack's sister, a thin, brown-haired girl, was bridesmaid. Outside the church an old woman shook Peter's hand. She crushed an empty confetti-bag in her own free hand. "The prettiest bride," she said, "that ever walked down the aisle. Yourself, God bless you, you're lookin' well. It won't be long now. Sure Jack and Mary might have waited and you'd have tied the knot for them."

He escaped, angry and mortified, from her grip and slipped into one of the cars. Why in hell hadn't he stayed in Dublin, or dumped the black clothes and bought a new suit that would, like the blast of a trumpet, have proclaimed the truth to the neighbours? He hadn't the money to buy a new suit. He hadn't the means of earning money. Then to cast the black clothes immediately would hurt his mother, as if he wanted to escape with one wild gesture from all the things she had imagined for him. He remembered her joy when she had bought him that first black suit. She sat beside him in the car, silent, not reproaching him, very erect and very frail, her faded face, her hair escaping in wisps from under her new hat. She was giving her daughter away, with sorrow but willingly. That was the lot and the destiny of women. In her grandchildren the world would begin for her all over again, faltering weak voices, tiny hands. But some men, the chosen, had a higher way to follow, greater sacrifice, greater reward. She had made the sacrifice, willingly and with joy. She had prayed in vain. The offering was returned, unaccepted. She sat silent and straight and did not blame him. He knew his own mind. God knew.

The excitement of the wedding gave him a chance to hide, sinking into his chair when the grace had been said before breakfast, absently seeing through the hotel window the pillared front of the courthouse, the ugly Boer War monument where a corpulent bronze woman offered a bronze wreath to dead, forgotten soldiers. His neighbours talked busily with their neighbours, forgetting him. He picked his food, heard Davy's honest voice, his loud laughter. The war was good. Weddings were good. People were so busy doing things, so excited by action, that they didn't notice the shame of the man who had stopped doing.

"Rita, you look solemn," said Davy. "Do weddings frighten you?"

She said: "Other people's weddings." The guests, with the readiness of wedding guests, accepted all things as wit. They laughed. Peter saw her for the first time. She hadn't been in the church. He remembered that she was some distant relation of Jack Carney—the long-tailed families in little towns. She sat near Davy, and Davy passed her plates and plates, lavishing attention on her with an obvious, good-natured air of interest that angered Peter.

She said: "I love weddings in April and May."

A voice said : "Why?"

The table shook with laughter. Peter watched the bronze woman, cursed the guests for fools.

"Rita's getting poetic," said Davy.

"Peter will tell you why," she said.

He hardened himself: his shame in crowds his solitary pride; never quote poetry to an unknown audience; lunacy to quote poetry to wedding-guests who want broad jokes about fur coats and little troubles.

"Please, Peter," she said.
He said bitterly, spitefully:

> "The valiant prime of the day
> And the dauntless youth of the year,
> When nothing that asks for bliss,
> Asking aright . . ."

A voice said it was time to cut the cake. He went on:

> ". . . is denied;
> And half the world a bridegroom is
> And half of the world a bride."

"My, what a memory," said Jack's mother.
"What's it mean?" said a little, dark, rotund girl.
"It's poetry," said Davy, solemnly.
Peter met her eyes, seeing there a sympathy and pity that he suddenly hated, looking through her until he saw Dowdall sitting on the shattered tree-stump, doubt and perplexity in his eyes. Then Dowdall was lost in the crowds going up and down before a city cinema under the white lights. Then there was only the bronze woman endlessly offering laurels to unresponsive soldiers.
When the guests crowded into the lounge he shook hands with Rita. She said : "What should I say?"
"Welcome home."
"Don't sneer."
"I wasn't sneering."
"I'm sorry, Peter. I'm glad to see you and you are welcome. But . . ."
"But what ?"
"I know how you feel."
"A failure."
"No, don't say that. You haven't failed. You couldn't fail. You knew your own mind and you did the right thing."
They walked away from the guests to the bay-window, looking

down the sloping street, looking up at the towering pillars of the courthouse.

"Do we ever know our own minds?" he said. "I took your advice. You knew more about it than I did."

"God forgive me."

"I knew you were right when I saw my own difficulties in another man."

A military lorry tugged up the hill, turning to the left under the shadow of the great pillars. He turned his back on the window.

"We'd better go back to the guests, Rita. We'll give scandal to the good people."

She said absently, seriously, in a way that startled him: "It would really be scandal now."

"What do you mean?"

"You see, Peter, a month ago Davy asked me to marry him. I think he's told your mother."

"Told her what?"

"That I said I would. Peter, what could I do? What was I to do?"

He looked at her and beyond her, seeing a twisted mixture of wildly incongruous things: Dowdall hunched in the steep gallery of a theatre, a red-headed girl with good knees, a bed of red flowers, the narrow face of his confessor bending to him in kindness, then dancing away on a spinning gramophone record. The guests were eating cake and drinking wine. Jack and Mary in the centre of the circle showed flushed, laughing faces. The red blossom coming to fullness, deep vermilion of the rose, sheltered and sanctified in the holy garden.

III

They missed Mary in the home. She had been light and laughter, cheery conversation, the intimate criticism that every brother needs from his sister. In her place was Peter sleeping in her room, to Davy a negative presence that he had suddenly and inexplicably commenced to dislike. With her went her chattels: the picture of a Norwegian fjord that she had always claimed as her own, the ornaments, the manicure set, the flapjack that had lain on her dressing-table. The room was no longer sacrosanct, the preserve of an intangible, mysterious femininity.

Peter felt it. Making his final decision he had thought of Mary. She would be there, laughing, attending, understanding, masking her pity in an affectation of equality, a say-as-I-please sisterhood. He had not imagined this emptiness. His father went to work, came from work, killing the last year that came between him and retirement, sinking deeper into the silence of age. His mother quietly did the duties of the house, never reproaching him. Davy came noisily from his labour, shouting and singing as he shaved at the mirror in the kitchen, trying to fill with empty sound the emptiness he felt like a pain.

"Peter the hermit," he said, "come out with me to the class to-night and take the scowl off your face."

Peter wearily closed his book. He said "No."

"Why?"

"I don't want to."

"Not good enough for you. Not intellectual enough."

"You said it. I didn't."

"You've got so used to sitting in the chimney-corner."

"Davy," the mother said. She tidied her brown hair, preparing to go visiting with her husband. "That's not a Christian thing to say."

"Well, it's the truth. Peter knows he can't sit acting the gentleman for ever."

"I've written to a chap I know in Dublin. He'll get me a job on a paper there. He promised."

"What's a promise? Small chance you have with paper disappearing off the face of the earth."

"His father has influence."

"He'll need it. You want to escape from the wee town, I suppose."

"Would you blame me?"

"To bigger horizons. Wider fields for your abilities."

Their father turned as he went into the hallway, came suddenly out of his quietness: "Davy, you might try to learn some manners at your class to-night. Peter never gives us any trouble in the house. When he goes out at night we don't have to fear that the next place we'll see him will be behind the bars."

"If he didn't give trouble he never gave anything else."

"He hasn't spent much of your money, Davy."

"He won't get the chance."

The father went out after his wife, slamming the door behind him in a quick stab of caged anger. Peter went on reading. Davy hunched himself for a while beside the red glow of the range, then walked across the kitchen into Peter's room. Peter listened, heard him shuffle on the floor. He said "What are you at in there?"

"Mind your own bloody business."

Peter tiptoed across the kitchen, flung the door open and looked in at Davy kneeling on the floor at the foot of a chest of drawers, holding in his hands a small parcel. "Busybody," said Davy, standing up, straightening his collar, nursing the parcel.

"What have you got there?"

"Wouldn't you like to know? Look!"

He peeled off the covering paper, showed a holster and revolver, a box of cartridges.

"Does it frighten you, Peter? Isn't it lovely?"

"A lovely thing to have in another man's room if the police came raiding."

"Mary didn't mind."

"Did she know it was there? Anyway, it doesn't matter which room it's in. It's under the roof. What effect would it have on Mother if the police came and found that?"

"You're considerate all of a sudden."

Davy buttoned his overcoat, reached for his hat. He said: "You weren't so considerate when you left the college." Peter turned his back, staring into the red range, feeling anger burning red in his own soul: the crude stupidity of Davy, too stupidly honest to hide his unreasoned jealousy. He said: "Leave that stuff at the Gaelic class."

"Who says?"

"I do. I'm older than you. I've got some sense."

Anger flamed up hot in him, parching his mouth. Davy went to the door. He said: "Go to hell." Peter gripped him, wheeled him around, forced him down against the stairs. Davy struggled, cursed, trying to free his arms, knowing the white determination of his brother for the strength of ten men. "You fool, you damned fool," Peter gasped, pressing his thumbs down on Davy's throat, choking him into helplessness. He stood up with the parcel in his hand and waited for Davy to come weakly to his feet.

"I was taking it out to-night at any rate. Why in hell can't you leave me alone?"

"Get out."

Davy looked at the white face, the red, angry lips, a little trickle of blood on the chin where teeth had bitten in vicious anger. He went out, banging the door in futile protest. Peter waited until the sound of his brother's steps had died away, until the anger burned itself out in him, leaving him cold and miserable, crouching down to the fire to feel its alien external warmth. Then he put on his hat and coat, turned down the gas and went out into the dark street, the parcel under his arm. He thought with bitter irony that if a policeman stopped and searched him that lunatic parcel would be worth at least five years. Outside the courthouse he rubbed shoulders with the military sentry. The doors were sandbagged now, the great ballroom that was part of the building made into a billet. Under the pillars he heard the whispering and laughing of soldiers and girls. The sentry was watchfully nervous, thinking of Norway, desiring the fun under the shadowy pillars. Peter felt an insane desire to dump the parcel at the sentry's feet, to run off into the darkness. He went up River Lane laughing at his own passing madness. There were two new shops in River Lane, two eating-houses for soldiers, sending out smelly heat and boisterous singing. There always had been new shops in River Lane, mushroom shops, closed and abandoned after a few months. Beyond the second eating-house the lane humped over a great bridge. He leaned on the parapet listening to the noise of the black, deep water sucking around the arches, watching the great bulk of the church spires vague against the night sky. The parcel was before him on the flat stone. He pushed it from him, startled by the suddenness with which it vanished, by the single distant splash. He stayed on the bridge watching and thinking. Two policemen came up out of the darkness, stared at him, walked on. From the military camp that Davy had helped to build soldiers rattled past to the cinema. Girls laughed. Civilians passed soft-footed in anonymous night. The blackness pressed down on him, crushed him. His soul was lost in a miserable river that flowed always in abominable night. He had changed Davy's good nature to pitiable, evident jealousy, to futile anger; his mother's joyful expectancy to patience without hope or promise of hope. This town in the watered plain circled by hills had nursed him and sent him forth, had hidden itself from him, the failure, in night. He could never see again the landmarks he loved. The river flowed on, bitterness without end, hiding its secret, and, without end, gloom.

IV

In Dublin in Mountjoy gaol a man died on hunger-strike. Davy read the newspaper aloud at breakfast, commented with a bitterness that seemed directed at the unmoved Peter. The world was shaking around them, men dying suddenly and terribly in twisted, frozen Norwegian seas, clinging desperately to stony shores. What was one life more or less? The poor died of hunger, martyred by the general consent of society, closed out from warmth and food. In Belfast a dance-hall was burned down. Two detectives were shot in Dublin. Davy leaned across the table and said: "That's the stuff to give them." Peter was silent. Since they had quarrelled that was Davy's only attempt at conversation: to read newspaper headlines, to comment truculently, baffled by Peter's quietness.

May came. Davy's face was radiant. "My God they rise early," he said. "They're in Belgium and Holland."

The streets of the town were vibrant with the news. Laden soldiers tramped to the railway station and were rolled off into the unknown. Luckier soldiers still slung along in irregular ranks, banging mugs and plates, cheerfully whistling German military music. "Haven't even tune of their own," said Davy. The grey Calvinistic houses came to life. The sons of those houses drilled and dressed in uniforms, built strange, awkward barriers of sandbags at the most unpractical points on all the roads leading from the town into the fresh, flowering countryside. Walking with Jim Carson along one of those roads in the May dusk Peter watched a regiment new to the town march in from the station. They sang and shouted. A small crowd gathered and cheered. Girls waved their hands. Carson said: "God help us. Irish girls wave welcome to the army of occupation."

"That was the voice of my brother Davy," said Peter.

"It's the truth."

"Maybe. Can we blame them? Men are scarce. What those girls feel is more powerful than nationality. It was before the nations of Europe were heard of. Deirdre or red Grainne would have waved to any man going into battle."

"Sometimes," said Carson, "I wonder at you. You're a painful old cynic."

"Cynicism is a refuge for the man who fails."

"You're no failure, Peter. You haven't even begun yet. You've any amount of ability and the whole world before you. Shape it as you want it."

"Is it worth shaping?"

"Balderdash," said Carson, and they went home through the dusk.

A letter came from Dowdall. Peter read it at the littered after-dinner table while his father and Davy looked through the window into the street, watching soldiers march past. The music of the pipes came up thin and jaunty over the sound of tramping feet.

"Are they goin' or comin', Davy?"

"Goin', Pa. Fusiliers. Irish fellows. There's Peter Mullins. His wife told me they were waitin' to be shifted to France."

The letter said there was good hope of a job some time during the summer. Dowdall himself had gone back to work, not in the bank but in an insurance office, dreading a new beginning with the old faces, the old discarded routine.

At the window Davy said: "Too late to shift them now. Even Peter Mullins couldn't help France, not if the Maginot Line goes."

"God help us, Davy, can't you find something else to talk about?" The mother bent over the range waiting for the washing-up water to heat.

"It's news, Mother, great news. There wasn't the like of it since the Roman Empire fell."

Peter said dryly: "When did that happen?" Davy flushed, ignored Peter, went on rhapsodically.

"It'll change the world, Mother. Change our lives and give freedom to Ireland. The weight will fall off from the shoulders of humanity."

"Where did you hear that, Davy? Radio Hamburg?" Davy flushed again, watching his pale, smiling brother sitting at the table, folding the crisp letter back into its envelope.

"There must be a big weight on your own shoulders, Davy, or you wouldn't feel so hot about it."

Davy put on his jacket and cap, went silently out to his work. The father turned from the window, kindled his pipe, lost himself in the newspaper. The mother carried the steaming kettle to the pantry, tumbled soiled dishes into hot water, rattled and washed. Peter wondered now at the silence of Davy. A month previously, a taunt would have provoked him to wild gesticulation, vehement argument. They had drifted away from each other, separated by something that neither of them would acknowledge. He could no longer help his brother. He could no longer understand his brother.

V

Coming home from Mary's house Peter heard the first aeroplane droning past, lost somewhere in the hot darkness of the night. Mary's house was a refuge. She understood and sympathised, laughed at his troubles until they dwindled and became part of the past, until he forgot the one misery that he could not tell even to her. But out again in the darkness the sense of his own failure came back to him. The men who fished for trout on the river below the town had a superstition, one among many, that the fisherman who missed his first rise had bad luck from the beginning of the day to the end of the day. Once a failure, always a failure.

The plane passed. The noise died away into the distance. A few doors and windows opened. Heads looked out into the darkness of Dublin Street. He felt all the discomfort of warm beds where sweat oozed from bodies and sheets wrinkled and roofs gave out the heat burned into them by the day's sun. Sleep would be impossible. The mind would turn restlessly, projecting horrid visions into the darkness. God, how pitiably he needed some positive motive to tire his mind and body, leaving him nights of sleep in honest weariness.

He turned up Devlin Street and passed his father's house. There was no sign of life about the closed door and the blind, black windows. He followed the street past the silent creamery, chalk-white in the darkness; under the dark railway arch, up the steep road until the cool peace of the fields was all around him, the town somewhere below in the shadows. A summer moon came up, showing suddenly the vague shape of mountains away beyond the river, then catching and glinting on the roofs of the town, on the straight steeples. He stood and watched, leaning against a stone gate-pillar, until his own unenviable identity melted into the night.

He might have been a tree or a bush or a stone pillar, dull, inanimate, fortified for ever, summer or winter, against the possibility of failure.

The second plane passed. He heard the jerky beat of the engine, the uneasy moving of a tired heart in the dark sky. A great shadow drifted across the moon, vanished again. Then with the suddenness of a man swinging a sword a great blade of light went stabbing and searching into the darkness. A gun exploded, something whistled and crashed and echoed in the hollow sky, melted into a shower of futile sparks falling and fading. Some poor, half-sober German lad had lost his way, startled a little town out of its monotonous slumbering and rising. The blade of light was gone but the town was awake. Shrill whistles sounded again and again in the dark streets, isolated cries, gathering and swelling into a confused murmur laughably resembling the swarming of bees, coming up the road towards him. He climbed over the gate, sheltered behind the deep hedge, watched them pass: a few old people in genuine alarm, the respectable middle-aged, the hilarious young, running from cramped streets where they sensed danger. He saw in comic vision the whole world in revolt against sweaty beds, against quiet and easy respectability, running wildly into the lawlessness of the fields. For ten minutes the road was crowded, then only a few stragglers went walking past at their ease. He climbed back over the gate, joined two men who were walking together.

"Evacuation, me eye," said one of them. "Downright bloody tomfoolery."

"Anyway, he's well back to Germany by this time," said the other. "If those daft soldiers hadn't fired off the gun I'd be asleep."

"A bad night for sleeping. It's too hot. We might as well go on and see the sport in the quarries."

They walked on. Peter walked with them. They wore dungaree suits and soiled cloth caps. Their talk was slow and sibilant, the accent of the lake country between Enniskillen and the western sea, an incipient brogue: workmen who had come to the town for the military contracts, a big dark man, a small, wizened, bald man who chewed and spat.

"There was one oul one," said the big man, "out in her shift, peltin' along the street an' she barefooted, cryin' out murdher."

"What under God will they do if they ever get a real air-raid?"

They overtook three women, two girls who helped an old woman up the mounting slope of the road.

"Give you a hand, granny?" said the bald man.

"God bless you, Jamesy, it'll be welcome."

He passed an arm around her, half-carrying her along the road. She wheezed her gratitude. The girls giggled, eyed Peter and the big man with eyes of speculation.

"Thank God for the Germans," said one of them.

"'Tisn't often we have an excuse for getting loose at this hour of the night."

She went up the road with the big man, leaving Peter with the second girl. He knew her by sight, eighteen-year-old, fair-haired, strong and shapely. He had noticed her a dozen times about the town, always with soldiers, chatting to them in the daytime, snuggling with them in the darkness in the doorway of a deserted shop in Dublin Street. Her eyes went over him, examining him in the moonlight, noticing with distaste the lack of brown battledress, belt or buckle. Still, a man was a man. She took his arm as they walked. Somewhere above another engine droned, menacing and powerful, whizzing propellers cutting and driving through the darkness. She ran in sudden fright, pulled him sideways off the road into the deep shadow of the ditch. He sat patiently on the damp grass, thick whitethorn over his head, listening to the beat of the engine going on and on towards the sea, watching the whiteness of her face and hair luminous in the shadow.

"God almighty," she said, "I coulda sworn that was another Jerry."

"Maybe it was."

"No fear. It was a Britisher. I know the sound of them."

She sat on the grass close beside him, and with a mechanical, melancholy sense of what was expected of him he put his left arm about her shoulders. She laughed softly, melting towards him, uniform or no uniform.

"You're a queer one, Peter Quinn."

"Queer?"

"You have left the college, haven't you? A body, couldn't be sure an' you still wearing that black suit."

"It's my own business. But I have left."

"No interference, you know. But they say the girl that ever drew a student away from his calling never had another good day."

He wanted to laugh, to bellow with laughter, but some instinctive regard for her quaint attempt at self-protection kept him silent. "You take no risks," he said. "But you needn't be afraid. You didn't draw me away from my calling."

She said suddenly: "Who did?"

"Nobody."

"That's not what they say in the town."

"Who says what?"

"It not my business, but nobody can help hearing wee bits o' gossip."

"About what ? The people would do well to mind their own affairs."

"God help you, they'd die if they had to do that. Or bust maybe, keepin' the words in."

"What did they say?"

She was suddenly secretive, smiling and mocking, hoping to draw him on into an intimacy where she could tell him as friend to friend, what the people were saying. He stood up.

"You're not going?"

"We'll get our death in this damp ditch."

"It's no damper than the quarries that they're all scooting to. Is that where you're heading for?"

"I'm going home to bed."

"Bed?" she tugged at his coat. "When was bed ever like this? Come on, Peter Quinn. Kiss me."

He balanced somewhere between disgust and mockery. Then her upturned face moved within him a force of perilous pity for the common coin, passed from one uniformed hand to another, hoping also for the great love, the honourable love. He kissed her. She drew in her breath, strangely content, the odour of cheap scent about her neck.

"Boy," she said, "you've got technique." Great Hollywood spoke in her voice.

"What's technique?"

"Some fellows kiss you all over your face."

"Do they?"

"That's because they don't love you. They're just out for what they can get. I know one soldier though. Wee Taffy they call him.

Taffy was a Welshman, you know, and Taffy was a thief. He says he loves me. Every single time I meet him, if there's nobody listening. Wants to marry me too. Me the happy wife. Isn't it a laff? He says, 'Do you love me, Josie?' and I say, 'Yes, Taffy.' The poor wee fellow. You couldn't hurt him, you know. But I don't love him all the same. He was a coal-miner before the war."

She snuggled closer to him, talking and talking, the meaning trickling out of her words, leaving them light and empty like inflated balloons.

"Peter Quinn, did you ever kiss anybody you loved?"

"I did. A long time ago."

"What did it feel like? Was it very different from kissing me?"

The laughter came in spite of himself. "It's not the kiss makes the difference, Josie. That's an external action like combing your hair or blowing your nose. But the love inside you changes the kiss into something a million times more than a kiss."

"That's education," she said thoughtfully. "They say you were the smartest boy ever went to the Brothers School."

"You seem to know plenty about me."

"I love knowing other people's business. It must be great to be clever. Or to love somebody that's clever."

She sneezed suddenly, pitifully shivering closer to him as the damp cold went into her limbs. The thin inadequate clothing moved under the fingers of his left hand. He stood up, gently drawing her to her feet.

"Leave me as far as the quarries," she said, "an' then go home to your beauty sleep."

They went up the road together. She leaned on his arm, silent, going back into her shell of detached, calculating hardness, half-ashamed of herself for condescending to a civilian. A lane cut at an angle from the road went upwards under heavy drooping hedges. Then the hedges dwindled, the lane topped a hill and left them suddenly on the edge of the old cutting, dropping steeply away from them into shadow. Beyond the shadow little figures moved, black in the moonlight. The babble of excited voices rose up.

"Down there," she said, "we'll separate. You won't want to get a bad name."

"Who cares?"

"I do. You wanta have sense, Peter Quinn. I'm not your class.

Besides, the lassies would say you left the college on account of me. An' if Taffy heard it he'd never forgive me."

She laughed, running away from him on the steep path that twisted down the face of the cutting. Her white head vanished into the shadow. He moved towards the path, hesitated, then sat down on a flat stone. Down below, against all regulations, somebody kindled a fire. A dozen voices sang together around the flame. The fun of it, the thrill of being a refugee on a night in May with absolutely no danger. He watched the little dark figures crowd around the fire. He listened to the singing. The path turned white as the moon moved round, the white head, the willing lips. That way lay relief, an end to this miserable tension. A dozen times his mind was almost made up. But he didn't take even the first step that would bring him to find her down there in the black, singing crowd around the flames.

When he stood up to go home he saw the couple for the first time, not more than twenty yards away, standing quietly in the shelter of a ditch. There was no mistaking the shape and figure of Davy, and when he thought who the girl must be he went weak with hopeless anger. Davy might say: "You keep good company, Peter." Davy always said the obvious thing. If he said that, Peter wondered would he strike him, his brother? At that moment he viciously hated Davy, the square face, the short, crisp hair, the unintelligent good nature. He was walking past pretending to ignore them as he would ignore any pair huddled in a ditch, when Rita called him by name.

"Hello, Rita," he said, "you keep bad hours." There was no answering jibe from Davy. Rita said "Peter, I want to talk to you." He walked over to them, wondering at the way they stood, awkward and apart from each other.

"Were you frightened by the planes?" he asked. Davy sullenly said "No." "Peter," Rita said, "Davy's in trouble."

"In trouble. What for?"

"The police," said Davy. "They raided the house to-night when you were out. I got out the back and hid in Rita's place. When the rush started we got outa the town. I can't go back."

"Why not? Did they find anything, arms or papers?"

"No. Damn the thing. But they've got something on me. Something big. It wasn't my fault, Peter. I was led into it. I didn't know under God what it was all about until it was done."

The voice quivered. Peter was torn with pity. Poor Davy, the loud words, the resounding empty pot, hadn't the sting of a revolutionary in him. Just good nature hidden in theatrical blood-and-thunder.

"God, knows this is cheerful news. What did you do?"

"I didn't do it. I didn't know. I was just there."

"Where?"

"Ballyclogher village. At the bank."

"Christ in Heaven. There was a man killed there."

"I didn't do it."

"Who did?"

"Look, Peter. I can't tell."

"Who killed him ?"

"Dick Slevin. Peter, it happened this way. Slevin came to me about three weeks ago. He said, 'Davy, there'll be a job on Saturday next—will you come?' I wanted to know what the job was. He said, 'A foraging expedition,' and I said, 'O.K.' I didn't know what he meant. A fortnight from last Saturday he picked me up in a car. He had two other fellows, one of them driving, strangers. I never laid eyes on them before. We drove to Ballyclogher, Slevin sitting beside me in the back. When we were driving into the village, in the morning, mind you, in broad daylight, he pulls a brute of a loaded Webley from under the seat an' sticks it into my fist."

The singing came up louder and louder over the edge of the cutting. Rita said: "Some people have all the fun." Davy's breath stuck and rasped in his throat.

"I began to get the wind up. I asked him what it was all about. He laughed and said it was a money operation. We drove up the village and halted at a corner a few yards away from the bank. Slevin said to me, 'Now's the time to do your stuff.' He told me to put the Webley into my pocket and cross the street right opposite the bank. When a two-seater car pulled up at the bank I was to come up behind it with the gun in my fist. I didn't know what in hell to do. I couldn't say 'No.'"

"Why couldn't you ?."

"God, Peter, you don't know Slevin. I couldn't refuse. I crossed the street. They was nobody about. Not many at any rate. But somebody must have seen me. In five minutes the car came up with two men inside and one in the dickey. Then a man got out with a brown bag in his hand. Slevin was on the pad before him. He had a tommy-gun in his hands. I never saw it until I saw it in his hands. The man with the bag pulled a gun out of his pocket but he hadn't a chance." Slevin got the bag. I ran for the car. I dropped the Webley in the middle of the street. Slevin pitched the bag to me an' opened up again with the tommy. The man in the dickey fell into the street and crawled around the corner to shelter. There was blood dripping out of him. The other fellow got the wind up an' stepped on it. We raced like hell outa the place. There wasn't a sinner to be seen."

He leaned back weakly on the slope of the ditch. The singing in the quarry died away, renewed itself to new rhythm and new words. Peter said: "This place isn't too safe. That fire will draw the police sooner or later." They walked down the lane towards the road. She slipped a hand around an arm of each of them, drawing them together again.

"Now that you've struck your blow," said Peter, "what under God do you intend to do?"

"Hide out with Jacob. Slevin's there."

"Tell me your company."

"That's not kind," said Rita. "Slevin led him into it."

"Slevin's as good as he is. Better. He's got courage. You can't lead a man into anything he doesn't want to go into."

"The harm's done now, Peter. There's no use in preaching."

"I'm not preaching, Rita. Gave up all idea of preaching a few months ago."

She took her hand away from his arm. At a gate into the fields Davy halted.

"There's a short cut this way to Jacob's place. It's better than gaol."

"And what then?"

"Maybe I'll get a chance to nip across the border. I know people I could hide with. It'll blow over some day."

He climbed up out of the hedge-shadow to sit a-straddle on the gate, his face white in the moonlight, the moon slipping down and down towards the meadows.

"I'm sorry, Peter," he said.

"No need to apologise to me. You're the sufferer. And our parents. They've been disappointed in both of us now. You the bread-winner. Me the priest."

"I'm sorry all the same, Peter."

"Go on, man. Go on and have sense. Take care you're not caught. I'll slip out to see you some time."

"Be careful then."

He dropped down on the other side of the gate, waved his hand, ran across the moonlit grass until the shadow of the hedges swallowed him again.

"An affectionate farewell," said Peter.

"Don't be horrible. He doesn't know what he's doing."

They walked together towards the town. She pushed her hands deep into the pockets of her dark trench-coat, her head down.

"Were you engaged, Rita?"

"He just asked me to marry him. I said I would. "He's good and generous."

"Is that everything?"

"It's a lot. It would never lead us to do anything wrong."

"Wrong?"

"Peter, I wasn't fair to you. I just wanted ..."

"Wanted what?"

She didn't answer. He said: "You were right, Rita Keenan. You said you loved me. I loved you too, all the time. You helped me to see it."

"Stop, Peter. It isn't right."

"The shoe's on the other foot now."

"I've given my word."

"So had I. At least I made a resolution and broke it."

"Stop. Stop."

"I won't stop. I'm telling the truth now."

She broke away from him when he put his hand on her arm, running under the railway arch, up the hill past the white creamery. He moved to follow her, then halted sick with hopelessness that was half anger. There was no female awkwardness, no mark of high heels and restraining skirts in the way she ran. He listened to the sound of her feet, seeing a white head go down the path into the shadowy pit of all old quarry cutting, wondering was it all nightmare, the wild visions of a mind shut out for ever from the day.

VI

In the morning the sun lived in the lake water like a million points of white fire. At noon the heat steadied the water into a single polished sheet. In the evening the last red path of light burned straight across the lake, touching the shore before the house, searching through the dirty window-panes into the kitchen with the rumpled outshot bed, the sagging bags of meal. The daily passage of the sun was the only thing that connected him with the normal life of normal men. Beyond the lake and over a few miles of fields the routine of the town went on: people walking to Mass along the cool morning pavement, men hurrying to work, hard boots to labour, soft boots to office and shops. The traffic of the day blocked Dublin Street, farmers' carts parked awkwardly outside shops, military lorries and gun-carriers thundering past, soldiers swaggering from billets to eat in the grey barracks, huge sable policemen stepping along the pavements as if they owned the town right down to its ancient foundations. Sunday was dull and quiet, but very peaceful and very holy from Mass to Benediction. If the war hadn't silenced the bells he could have heard them over the fields and over the water. It might all have been a million miles away, on the other face of the moon, in another universe.

The hut was a prison, worse than a prison. In Belfast gaol he would have had good company, lads with ideals. They had a Gaelic class there or they learned Gaelic separately or they did something or other, he wasn't sure what.

The endless rattle of the water on the beach of stones irritated and confused him, entangled his ideas. The lake looked so cool, so heavenly cool when the sun was high, when the light of day kept them in the house looking through the window at the other shore. Townspeople bathed there, off a wooden jetty that stepped out over the cool green water, with thin diving-boards shooting white bodies into the air to fall again with an audible splash. In the nights he would go down naked to the water, stepping carefully on the stones, wading out until the thrust of the little waves swung him into softness and delicious coolness. Still, it was uneasy pleasure. Slevin said it was insanity. A chance discovery was as good or as bad as any other discovery. God only knew what prowling idiot might see him swimming naked in the night.

"You won't get a second chance if you're caught," Slevin said. "You were there when a man was killed."

But the pleasure was worth the risk : the feeling of escape, of instant detachment from Slevin, giggling and unshaven, from the imbecilic Jacob with the monstrous unfastened boots, drifting every day deeper into grinning, gesticulating incoherence. Deep in the water, swimming easily in the shadow of the trees, the whole enormity of what had happened slipped away from him. He was a boy again, shutting out all care from the snugness of a warm bed with wind bullying the chimney and rain whipping at the window. No clean beds now. Slevin would soon be as bad as Jacob.

The prospect of the coming winter sickened him. Short cold days and long dark nights spent huddled around the smoky hearth, watching the faces of Slevin and Jacob, three animals in one cave. Slevin had given up all pretence to slick neatness. His black hair bunched uncombed about the collar of his coat. He shaved seldom, boasted about his own power and his courage and the reward on his head as if they were all schoolboys playing gangs.

"God, Davy," he said, "if you walked into the town and made yourself nice to the head constable you'd get off easy and have money to settle down on. I'm worth a good lot."

Davy kept his temper. "I wouldn't say that to a friend, Dick."

"An outlaw has no friend."

"Outlaw be damned. We're not outlaws."

"What are we then?"

"Soldiers."

"Soldiers of the republic, is it? Davy, you're twenty-five years out of date. There is an army in this country, in green uniforms, the army of Ireland. You should be there. I'm just a guy that didn't fit anywhere."

"Our country's divided. We could only do as we saw best."

"Don't be a mug. Not we. You. I'm different. You want to see Ireland free, whatever you mean by that. I don't give a curse. If Ireland were free to-morrow I'd be where I am, see? On the run. Fellows like me are always on the run."

"The cinema has gone to your head."

"I've always hated them.

"Hated who?"

"Those blackguards of police."

"So have I."

"But you hated them because they represented England. I hated them because they represented law, any law, see?"

When they talked or argued Jacob sat listening, his eyes dull with idiocy, moist lips gaping as if he swallowed every word to digest it like bread in some strange physical understanding. All day he doddered about the house, feeding the few hens that roosted in the black barn, looking after the one milch cow. In the corner between the hills and the lake the little farm returned to wilderness; meadow-drains clogged and the rain sent the swelling lake water seeping through the rank grasses; hedges towered into spreading thorny strength; cart-paths softened into mud until finally the grass devoured them. Jacob did the shopping, shuffling the few miles into the town, halting to stare vacantly over gates into the fields or to peer down drains carrying rainwater from the roads into the dykes. One evening Peter brought him back from the town.

"Keep your eye on this poor fellow," he said. "I picked him up nearly on the threshold of the police barracks."

Jacob shuffled to a seat near the window. Walking in the hot sun had beaded his little three-cornered forehead with greasy perspiration. He held his hands before him, nervously watching the nervous twitching of his fingers, like a child caught in a petty misdeed. Slevin crossed the kitchen and stood beside him.

"You squealing imbecile." His hand was raised to strike.

"I wouldn't hit him, Slevin," Peter said. "He's not responsible."

"Are you ordering me, Peter Quinn."

"If you like."

"I'm a dangerous man, Peter, to order."

Peter leaned back on the edge of the bed, relaxed into genuine laughter. "Are you pointing the gun at me, Billy the Kid ? Dick, I tanned you a dozen times when we were at school. I'll do it again if you lay a finger on him. It's his house. If you don't like it, get out.

Davy waited, tense with fear. Slevin crossed the floor and went out into the sun, across the street towards the black barn.

"You shouldn't provoke him, Peter. He's killed men."

"So could anybody with a gun. He won't use the gun on me. The quicker you clear out the better, Davy."

"I'll have a chance next week."

"Take it."

Peter crossed the stony beach to the lane on his way home. A shoal of feeding perch circled around two grey stones that came up to break the water and gather erratic swarms of flies. He watched the raised fins rippling the surface, the flash of white bellies and coloured sides. When he turned again Slevin was there blocking the middle of the lane.

"You insulted me, Quinn," he said.

"That's too bad."

"You'll apologise."

For the moment the weakness of gathering anger paralysed Peter, freezing his reason, showing him in the man opposed to him something as impersonal as a mathematical point, concentrating and relieving the restrained irritation of six months. He went forward. Slevin caught his shoulder and Peter struck and struck again, knowing the other man was fighting back, feeling his blows as puny things that touched only the remote outer shell of his anger. Then his head cleared and he saw Slevin lying by the edge of the water, his face marked and bleeding. He came slowly to his feet. Peter watched him, suddenly sick at his own brutality, filled with pity for the broken, hunted man.

"I'm sorry, Slevin. But, God, man, you angered me."

Slevin smiled, surprisingly. "I feel better," he said. "I bled you too, Peter. I feel like a schoolboy again. We've changed, haven't we, you and I? Both failures. I'm worse, though. I've blood on my hands."

He went back up the lane towards the house. Peter followed him for a few yards, then changed his mind and turned homewards again. The feeding perch passed out towards the deep water, leaping for the alert little flies splashing on the surface like handfuls of carelessly flung pebbles.

VII

All day long the June sun flooded into dusty streets, traffic rattled up and down, or out over the bridge on the road to Derry, or up the hill and past the cemetery on the road to Dublin. The same harelipped, shawled woman whined for alms in the cool church porch. The same loafer rubbed his greasy back against the same corner, held horses for shopping farmers who paid him in reluctant coppers. The sun danced in blue flame on the whirring wings of pigeons moving from roof to roof. The evening rooks fluttered in dusty argument in the trees around the priest's house.

Men there had accepted their values, were confident that nothing would change. A war might fill with soldiers the courthouse, the workhouse, the Orange hall, a few palatial and unmanageable private residences that would soon have been abandoned, war or no war. Railings might be torn down, to lie rusting in a scrap-heap at the bottom of the market-yard. An antiquated German gun captured in one war was carted away to be melted down as part of another war. Reservist corner-boys, with the hot thirst of Indian or Egyptian sun in their throats, went from the corners, marching off to France or Egypt or India or Burma. But no war could unsettle the values that the men of his town accepted. Peter watched them and talked with them, wondering at his own alien inability to fit into their scheme of things. In a sleepless night his soul was hungry for the rounded content of lives that began and ended in the flat land by the river, cradled by the smooth hills. But the bitter revelation of the sun disgusted him with his own acceptance, showed him the transparency of that content, and behind it the endlessly contorting agony of human souls everywhere the same, the same wants, the same inabilities.

The parish priest walked the street in the June sunlight: a tall, grey-headed man carrying his umbrella in all weathers, shading his eyes in the bent width of his hat-brim, followed by his great spotted dog. The people knew him: the priest, the priest's dog. He knew them, his people, his children, God's trust to him. That was the accepted relationship, the settled contract, agreed upon for centuries, even when his predecessor was a hunted, barefooted man reading Mass at a rock altar on the bare side of a mountain. He talked the flat demi-Scotch of the Bann Valley, practised the old ways that were strangely unsuited to the younger of his parishioners, questioned courting couples about their intentions, visited the houses, whistled for children, told them stories of fairies and fighting men. The young couples grew up from their tumbling on warm June grass, became respectable married people, raised children, placed the best chair for the priest when he came to visit them. Under the hat-brim the old grey eyes twinkled with fun, the comment of his mind on the delighted Sunday-morning face of the Church of Ireland minister watching his amazing new congregation of imported English conscripts forced by military discipline into church attendance. After the war the Church of Ireland would have its handful of zealots at Sunday service, except in July when the glorious and immortal memory sent the Orangemen to their knees. The customary hundreds would rattle past to the Catholic church, crowding through the great arched doorways under the tall spires. The world might change, but these things never would change.

The police visited the house again. His mother crossed the landing into Peter's room, shook him gently by the shoulder. She was frail and pathetic in her, long white nightdress, her faded hair hidden in something between a turban and a nightcap, her face pale with anxiety and fear.

"Will you come down to them, Peter? It doesn't fit your father at his age an' with his hasty temper. Pray God that nothing happens that would affect his pension."

He pulled on his trousers, went barefooted down the stairs into the kitchen and opened the door. They shuffled awkwardly over the threshold, a constable and two specials. The constable was called Jones, known to the town as Tinker Jones since the Christmas-eve night that a black-chinned Connaught tinker had beaten him unmercifully. The two specials were local Orangemen. One of them Peter had fought with when they were lads at school.

Jones said: "What's your name?"

Peter touched a match to the gas-mantle. He said:

"Ask your pal. He knows me since we were knee-high."

"It's not him," the special said. "It's his brother, Peter." He leaned his rifle against the table.

"You wouldn't know where the other fella is?" asked Jones.

"What other fellow?"

"No bloody lip. Your brother, I mean."

"I wouldn't."

"He wouldn't be in the house now, would he?"

"Search it if you like."

"I wouldn't think twice of it."

"Go ahead then."

The special picked up his rifle again, whispered something to Jones.

"You wouldn't have any ideas about freeing Ireland, would you?" Jones pushed his face close to Peter.

"Everybody has ideas. Have you any?"

"It's a waste o' bloody time," the special said. "You'll get nothing outa him. Anyway, the other fellow isn't next or near the place." He turned to Peter : "You know we could search the house if we wanted to?"

Peter smiled. "Alec, I hardly knew you. Do you remember the day I beat you in the corner of the fairgreen? Somebody told me you had joined the Army."

The man flushed. "I'm on home defence."

"Not as exciting at Dunkirk all the same, Alec. Out there you wouldn't have time to disturb your neighbours in the middle of the night."

He heard his mother's slippered feet on the stairs. She looked down at them, an old tweed coat wrapping her, the nightdress white below her knees.

"What in God's name do ye want? Isn't it enough that my son is wandering homeless?"

The specials shifted their feet uneasily. Jones took refuge in a ponderous official pose.

"Our duty, ma'am. Is your son Davy at home?"

"He's not."

"Where is he?"

"God knows."

"Does your other son know?"

"I said God alone knew."

"We'll take your word for it, ma'am. We won't search."

They turned out again through the tiny hallway.

"Don't let the light escape," Peter said. "One of the German fellows at Dunkirk might see it."

Jones grumbled. "You've too much talk. Ten to one you're a bloody rebel like your brother."

Peter slipped home the bolt, came back to the kitchen. His mother poked the fire, stirring life from black and brown embers.

"Go to bed, Mother. It's dead."

"You shouldn't provoke them, Peter. You know they have the power."

"Power isn't everything. Look at Alec, the lout. They talk loyalty and drum loyalty but they don't want the fighting to come any nearer than the Battle of the Boyne. It's the tattered papishes from the back lane that were lost at Dunkirk. Look at poor Francie Mulligan."

She went up the stairs ahead of him. "I know, son, I know. Still, there are decent men among them. And brave men."

"They're not too noticeable. If Winston Churchill had been a young man in this town he'd have joined either the British Army or the I.R.A. There's no half-way house for honest men."

She said absently: "Pray to your guardian angel. The I.R.A. are just misguided lads. Poor Davy. Poor Davy."

He lay in his bed, his window open to the quiet darkness. Poor Davy. Poor Davy. Poor Francie Mulligan. Francie was one of the men who came back. After the bomb dropped, a little boat had picked him up out of the waves and brought him back to England to hospital. He died there. Soldiering had been in his blood. His father was a soldier. Nobody knew which soldier. His mother drudged her consumptive way to an early grave, leaving Francie, tiny and grimy and tattered, running wild on the streets, growing up to a life of odd jobs, passing through a reformatory, graduating into a military barracks. He came back dead, a hero, a dead hero, to be buried in pomp, thin pipes wailing: "The Flowers of the Forest." Francie the Flower. Other men came back alive, greyfaced, their eyes dull with horror, not at all heroic.

Jim Stanley who had gone to school with Peter Quinn came to the house one day, his breath whetted with the tang of whisky, confusing his memories of schooldays, football games, classes, teachers' jokes, with red pictures of France: the canal where the grey hordes advanced somewhere north of Lille, the thunderous French guns, men in the chaos killing their own companions, the road to Ostend between the sea and the sand-dunes alive with German snipers. He had remembered geography lessons, Brother Kane dictating notes, a blackbird singing on the tree outside the window, the evening sun slanting across the convent field. Ostend in flames, bewildered refugees shouting on the roads. The way south to Dunkirk and out at sea the booming of British guns; the beach and the diving planes. When he was picked out of the sea he was wearing only a lady's jumper, an unknown lady. A sailor found time to make a joke heard above the screaming of the planes.

They came back out of horror and nightmares of dead men,

useless horror, wasted men, bewildered in life, heaped together in bewildered death. James MacFadden was two days at home nursing a wounded leg when his father had a letter telling him his son James had been lost in France. James, active in death, deserted across the border into Donegal. John Nolan remembered only grey men who roared as they ran. A young Welshman in the new camp battered and shattered his head with a brick. Taffy was a Welshman and Taffy was a thief. This was only the backwash of a great wave that had burst on the French shore, startling the great English cities into the terrible consciousness of danger but leaving them the pig-headed belief in their own power, yesterday, to-day and the same . . . No, that was blasphemous. To Caesar the things of . . .

He wrenched his mind back from the softness of sleep, inviting softness, deep and comforting and warm. Davy would rejoice, would mutter the name of Germany like a blessed incantation. The Orange special would sink into sullen reflectiveness, wondering had he after all backed a loser, feeling the bond between his own sense of superiority and the code of marching Prussia. This was Ireland, as absurd and entangled as the whole lunatic world, each man like each nation digging into the past for buried bitterness to anger him against his neighbour. Men died like cattle on the French shore doing incredibly heroic things to no particular purpose. Men sat in Belfast gaol, confined and guarded by their next-door neighbours, also to no particular purpose. Orange and Green lived like windy lizards on irrational generalisations, sighed dangerously for differing ideals, forgetting everything that should bind men together. God, what a mess and a muddle. All a muddle. All a muddle. A fragment of impossible Dickensian oratory danced in his head like an elusive, annoying bluebottle. Some honest man telling Joe Bounderby (how Dickensian!) that something or other was all a muddle. Love, and the things men tried to achieve, the quarrels they made, their sins and virtues, strengths and weaknesses, mixed without plan or pattern, a muddle, a maze. Two brothers loved one girl who loved one of the brothers and had given her word to marry the other. A good mother prayed that her son might go forward to the altar of God; and God, who gave joy to his youth, gave sorrow to the age of his mother. Or was it God's doing or his own weakness? Dowdall said they never would know. A foolish lad lost his way in generalisations and ideals, ended up a hunted, homeless wanderer, in company with another lad that bitterness had driven to kill, shutting him off for ever from the blackbird singing and the evening sun on the convent field, on a home like Jack Carney's home with Mary's red hair tossed radiant on the pillow, the red blossom, deep vermilion of the rose, sheltered and sanctified in the holy garden with the occasional white flowers, where cedar branches creaked outside the windows, where the ghosts of tall, dead ladies swept along empty corridors disturbing pale students kneeling at shrines, where vinous squires once slept it off in Greek temples, and a shattered Diana sneered after Actaeon running from the hounds into the land without light, without stars, into sleep, sleep, blessed sleep.

5

The Sea

I

WHEN Peter and Carson left the kitchen of John Mickey's house the whole assembly, visitors and people of the neighbourhood, had stopped dancing. They sat around the walls and rested. The tall, thin-faced fiddler and the lad from Belfast who played the piano-accordion were talking music in the corner between the red hearth and the doorway into the bedroom. Standing in the doorway an old greyhead, who had crossed the wet sand from Gweedore to the Rosses, began to sing in Gaelic. The song went back like a strong shaft of light, illuminating the centuries back to Bonny Prince Charlie, the broken people in Ireland dreaming of a leader as men in famine might dream of food. The song told about the great new law in France. It mentioned the grand old Duke of York. It spoke of Ireland as the woman of the house, patient and careful and worried about the rent. Everybody in the kitchen sang the chorus: asking the woman of the house what her trouble might be, telling her that henceforward she would live independently on her own land and pay no rent.

Peter closed the door behind him, muffling the singing. They went down the path between grey and speckled rocks, fields the size of a blanket, high, carefully built stone walls, to the cottage where Hudie lived, and his sister, and Cormac the father of Hudie, and little Hudie the adopted child. Beyond the cottage, the rocks, the little field, the tall stone walls went on down to the flat wet sand left bare by the tide. Beyond the strand was a peninsula of dunes gripped and held by the bitter bent grass, standing up to the blows of the great Atlantic. That tough grass was the last green fringe of Europe.

"They shouldn't sing those songs," Peter said. "They're bad enough in the heart of the country in the rich valleys, in the flat midlands, in shabby, beautiful Dublin, in black Belfast. But not here. This land is in agony. Those grey rocks. They're like steel when the moonlight catches them. That last fragment of Europe disturbs me like the thought of death and judgment. Then those old songs come raking and scraping like tongs in the embers, making us remember Cromwell, the hounding of our ancestors into these rocky places, famine, emigration."

"It doesn't do us any harm to remember things like that."

They rounded a sharp shoulder of grey rock. The path dropped suddenly. The music ended as if cut with a knife. Below them in the shadows around Hudie's house they could hear the grate of a sharpening-stone on steel.

"That's little Hudie," Peter said. "He's at that bill-hook all day."

"A blunt edge is better for catching the sand-eels."

"Tell little Hudie that. He'd laugh at you. He's like everybody else in Ireland, in love with the grindstone."

Carson sat down on a rock at the edge of the path. The distant rim of surf was like silver, frozen under the moon.

"Look, Peter boy," he said. "Do you see the college up there on the hill behind John Mickey's house?"

Peter saw it. He knew it inside and outside. So did Carson. In the morning four or five or maybe a dozen priests said Mass there. When the students, young and old, had eaten breakfast in the houses of the people they went back up the hill to the college: the long, grey walls, the latticed windows, the sloping slated roof.

For four or five hours every day they sat there on hard benches and learned Gaelic that had been spoken around those rocks since the light first broke on Ireland. No English was spoken in the homes of the people. No English was spoken under that roof of sloping slates. If you wanted to speak English the whole of Ireland was at your disposal: the cities, the towns, the cultivatable rural places, the seaside resorts with their little bit of Brighton and their faint, faint echoes of Atlantic City; all Ireland—except those acres of rocks and sand and miniature fields. You spoke Gaelic there or you got out. It was the rule of the men who had founded and who conducted the college. Carson did it because he believed in it. Peter did it because a journalist in Dublin might at some time in the future find the language useful. Anyway, it was a holiday; for after tea when the blackboards had vanished the people at the college danced until midnight; the national dances, the "Walls of Limerick," the "Waves of Tory." No jive, no jitterbug, not even a waltz. Dances that strong men had made for their own pleasure, before the art of amusement began to pay international dividends. It was fanaticism, Peter thought grimly, but, taken in conjunction with the sea, the sun, the great wind, the girls who came to the college, it was fun. After the dance the lights died in the little windows, the night crept out from the land to the sea, following the sun to Brooklyn. The dogs barked to each other from one house to the next, all along the coast, comforting each other in the darkness.

Peter saw it. He couldn't help seeing it on the hilltop, big and black with the moon behind it. There was no dance there that night on account of the dance in John Mickey's, on account of the crowd going out to dig the sand-eels on the tideless strand.

"Fifty years ago," said Carson, "the Irish people were forgetting that they had a language or a past, or national pride, or anything to distinguish them from other people . . ."

"Hold on there," said Peter.

"Shut up," bellowed Carson. "This is my turn. Here on my own ground, in Gaelic-speaking Ireland. I've listened to you long enough. You're the worm of doubt telling a man that he might possibly be wrong. You belong to the cities that are now mostly American. Or to the Six Counties that are neither British, American nor Irish. But this is Gaelic Ireland, and here Ireland speaks."

"You're welcome to it. You'll rear a hardy people on these rocks."

"Fifty years ago," said Carson, "the Irish people were ready to have their children rocked in English cradles. That's a metaphor." He guffawed his own pleasure in argument in Gaelic that left Peter at the mercy of a much more fluent speaker. Carson described Peter's state as verbal constipation.

"What was wrong with the English cradles?"

"Nothing. The best in the world for the children of English parents. For us the result would have been widespread national colic. Then a few men: poets, writers, scholars in folklore, in the words and relics of the past made people realise that Ireland could have no consistent, coherent future if Irish men and women were ignorant of their past. The very foundations of nationhood rested on such apparently trivial things as the remnants of bardic verse, the coloured songs of the country people. That wasn't the whole story. The people of a modern nation must take into account a million diverse things. But those songs, poems, stories and traditions were important. The language that enshrined them was important. It was a window into our own past. That was how the college came to be built, and other colleges like it in bare stony places by the Atlantic. The language lived there. The sheer cold poverty of those rocks had never meant anything to the enterprise of financial civilisation. So the tongue and the idiom of commercial civilisation stayed in warm, comfortable places: cities, towns, green valleys."

Peter clapped his hands, nasalised ironically: "For this is Ireland, land of unspoiled Gaels and migratory labourers."

"You're talking in English."

"I'm talking in American, the language of a great, more or less Irish people. Who won Bunker's Hill? The Ulster Presbyterians. Who fought the war of the States? The Irish. Who gave America her heavyweight boxers? The Irish. Who gave America her great entertainers? Why, the negroes and the Irish. An Irish Folklore Commission man recorded Gaelic folk-tales in the heart of Chicago. And all those people went to help build America for the simple reason that hunger drove them out of your Gaelic paradise."

"But what caused the hunger? English Rule."

"They're going still. Only now they go to England."

Below them the rasp of the stone on the steel of the billhook suddenly ceased. The moon moved out of a cloud. They saw the shadows of Hudie, little Hudie, the collie dog, move down the path by the edge of the cornfield towards the strand where the little eels were hiding.

"They're not waiting on us," Peter said.

"The tide's full out."

They passed the house and followed them down the path. Hudie brushed his moustache upwards from his lips with his right hand.

"There's a strand in it," he said.

"It isn't fully ebbed yet," said Peter, splashing through a half-inch depth of cool water where the path widened out on the sand.

"'Tis ebbed. The water lies here. There's a little stream comes down below Paddy Mickey's house."

The shore was behind them: the lights in the windows, the dogs barking to each other, the thin, distant sound of a fiddle in the house where the people were dancing, the pattern of stone ditches, the black bulk of the college. Weed-covered stones dotted the wet, flabby sand. The path bent this way and that way, under the shadow of the shore, past the swimming-pool and the point that was dangerous when the tide came cutting in from two different directions. Then it twisted out of the shadow into the moonlight, away from weeds and stones and flabby sand, out to lose itself in miles of strand that shone like silver. The collie ran, barking. Little Hudie ran, sinking his hard, bare feet in the richness of the beautiful sand. The running shadows flickered with a curious cinematic effect, on and on to the place where the people were gathered in scores, catching and bucketing the sweet sand-eels. They walked soberly towards that place: the little hollows scooped in the sand and holding the tide-water, feet splashing, dogs barking, men and women talking in accents as old as Homer. Hudie looked backwards.

"They built the swimming-pool in the wrong place," he said. "The tide takes the mud in there. The dirtiest corner of the shore. Still, it was a great job and a great man that ordered it to be done. He gave the people in this part a new spirit. When he came here the Gaelic was dying. The clergy didn't speak it. The shopkeeper didn't speak it. When you went to Scotland on hired labour it was the English you needed. In the school they taught no Irish."

"That's changed now."

"The whole world's changed," said Hudie. "The landlords are gone. We're proud of the Gaelic now. Stories and songs aren't the same in any other language. We've clean, slated houses now. He did it. The man who began the college. God rest him."

Hudie pushed his graip into the sand, turned it up quickly. Peter grabbed the thin, silvery body, dropped it into the bucket, where it beat hopelessly for a moment against the walls of its iron prison. Little Hudie uncovered an eel with his billhook, lost it again in the clear water of the pool. The graip flung up two more. Carson got his hand around one of them. Peter fumbled for a moment and the other had burrowed back into the sand. All around them men were digging, bending, grabbing, splashing in the pools, shouting and laughing with excitement. The people from the dance came out over the sand. Behind them was the shore, distant now and casting no shadow. Beyond the shore Peter guessed at the mountains, the flat back of Muckish, the cold pyramid of Errigal, the lakes and rivers and mountains of Donegal, the hills and valleys of Ireland, the coloured streets of Dublin and Dowdall in an insurance office, the blacked-out streets of Belfast and his own town, his father and mother, Mary with red hair, Rita with dark hair. All that seemed very far away. His world had compressed itself into that one patch of silver sand, and bending dark bodies of men and women. He was neither in Europe nor in America; but placed on the sand-eel strand, a vantage-point above the woes of Europe and the woes of men. It was escape.

Hudie waved his hand towards the low line of dunes corseted together with tough bent-grass.

"Beyond that," he said, "there's no stop until you're in New York. The Irish used to go that way in their thousands. They used say as a joke that Brooklyn was the next parish."

II

At nine o'clock in the morning Hudie's sister, the woman of the house, tapped the doors of their bedrooms, said it was time for the college. She really meant that it was time for breakfast. With the servant-girl she crossed the few yards of soft grass between the large new house where the visitors slept and the small old house where she and the girl, Hudie and old Cormac and little Hudie slept. She was small and red-cheeked. She pattered in soft slippers around the great kitchen of the new house, with one door closed against the wind and one door open to the sun. She shouted at the two dogs in quick, brittle Gaelic; laid the dining-table; kindled the fire in the modern range that had replaced the old open hearth. Then punctually at nine o'clock she tapped on the doors of the four bedrooms, called out that it was time for the college. The first class began at eleven o'clock. The clerical student from Armagh came up from his room where he had read quietly for twenty minutes after eight o'clock Mass. The little fair-haired teacher from Belfast came up adjusting his braces, pulled his shoes out from the space under the range, sat to lace them, on a low stool with his back to the wall. He sang snatches of songs, chatted with the woman of the house, smacked the servant-girl playfully as she bent over the range. They sat at the table eating and chatting. Outside the window the wind played with the little branches of a berried mountain ash. In those rocky places the eye hungered for trees, green colour against the grey, shade when the sun was shining; but apart from an odd mountain ash, or a whitethorn hedge twisted away from the wind, or the apple trees in the deep hollow behind Big John's house, there were no trees in the neighbourhood. So they talked and ate, feasted their eyes on the beauty of green leaves and red berries brilliant against the rising, rocky slope with its clean white houses; and the infinite blue sky above radiant with morning.

Peter and Carson ignored the summons and stayed in bed. Carson rolled over, grunted damnation on the college, relaxed after the weariness of walking on the sand and digging for the sand-eels. Peter in the front bedroom propped himself up with pillows, leisurely flicked the pages of half a dozen books piled on the table beside his bed. Learning Irish, not in school but from living people who spoke it as a living language, was not, he considered condescendingly, a waste of time. His condescension infuriated Carson, who spoke Irish as well as he spoke English, but, in his reading, left the poets of the past very much alone. Egan O'Rahilly, or O'Bruadair, or Red Owen O'Sullivan meant little or nothing to Carson. To Peter they were the first voices he had heard speaking authentically of a time and a scheme of things gone as completely as the snow of last winter. O'Rahilly lamented the ruin of the land of Fodla, the destruction that had overtaken the great families of Ireland. He might have found more notable matter for lamentation in the fate of the people left to rot leaderless through the eighteenth century. But even in that detachment displayed by the poet, in his bitterness, in his litany of the miseries that had come like plagues in his starless land, Peter found something sympathetic. He could not understand it. He was not complimented by it. He felt uneasily that sympathy with the deficiencies of a dead poet implied something lacking in himself. He heard a voice telling him that he was too proud to approach the altar of God.

He snapped the volume of verse shut, turned for escape to a volume of short stories by a modern author who had grown to manhood not more than a mile from Hudie's house. This man knew the place: the rocks, the spots of sweet grass, the lines of stone walls, the sea and the changing colours of the waves. He knew the storm in the night, the terrible calm of the morning after, broken fragments of a boat rocking on the oily water, dead bodies black on the beach, sorrow in a dozen homes. Above all he knew the people: the rake and the card-player; the cautious skinflint; the ancient, renowned for story-telling; the woman noted for dancing and sweet singing; the fighting and labouring in the potato-fields of Ayrshire. Any one of a dozen white-headed girls as common as blackberries in that place might have been in his mind when he described his heroine. He knew the songs of the place. Peter read out one verse. It talked about a man who had all the learning the Church could give him, but he bargained his faith for the sake of a woman.

Peter wondered bitterly did the man in the song really get the woman he had abandoned so much for. He closed the book and lay back in bed. Hudie's shadow flicked past between the sun and the blind. Hudie's hobnails grated on the smooth rock at the corner of the house. Hudie and Cormac were looking down at the sea and talking together. Cormac came out every morning, barefooted, wearing his sailor-cap and jersey with dark hard-cloth trousers. He would lean on his stick and stand at the corner of the house, looking down at the sea out of eyes withered with the passing of ninety years. Cormac could tell you about the shooting of Lord Leitrim, about the evictions in Gweedore when the policeman was killed and the priest arrested, about the emigrants walking down to the point, year in and year out, to catch the boat to Glasgow, or over the hills to Derry to catch the American liner. Year after year. The country bleeding to death ever since the proud, bitter poet lamented the misery of the land without stars.

At the window Cormac and Hudie talked. Their voices identified themselves with the wailings of a lost poet, with a randy song about the man who exchanged his faith for a woman. Did he get the woman? Or did the devil cheat him in the end? Dowdall said we never would know. No, that wasn't what Dowdall was talking about. Dowdall never mentioned a woman. Or did he? The voices at the window went backwards and faded. Dowdall was there talking Gaelic with an Oxford accent. Poor Dowdall. He never could catch the accent of the place. He didn't really belong there.

When he awoke Carson was sitting on the edge of the bed dusting fine sea-sand out of a tattered grey sock.

"Get up," he said. "It's dinnertime."

"Tell the girl to carry up my dinner."

"We've got visitors."

"Visitors be damned."

"Your brother Davy's one, and there's a lady along with him."

Peter slipped his feet slowly to the floor. He heard voices in the kitchen, but without listening he knew who the lady was. Anyway, she wouldn't be talking. She couldn't speak a word of Gaelic. Davy was talking to the servant-girl, to the woman of the house, to Hudie who came clattering in over the threshold. Davy came over often, walking the few miles from the farm back in the mountains where he lived with people he had known for years. He worked on the farm, did odd jobs for the people of the neighbourhood, passed unnoticed in that backward place. His visit was no surprise. But the lady? Peter was suddenly conscious that he was angry with her, coming to Davy, coming to the place at all. She knew he was there on holiday. She knew. Damn her, she knew more than was good for her, for Davy, for himself. She had no business there. She belonged to the town beyond the border. He splashed cold water on his face. She belonged to the darkness and to lost hopes. He knotted his tie, brushed his hair, followed Carson down to the kitchen.

She stood up and reached him her hand, but she didn't speak. She couldn't. There was that rule about speaking English in the houses. Davy in the chair by the window read yesterday's paper. He didn't stand up. Carson stood with his back to the range and began to sing. He caught the servant-girl round the waist and led her step-dancing up and down the kitchen. The tiredness of the night had gone out of his bones. The woman of the house laughed at the fun. Hudie and Davy began to talk about the war. Hudie said Hitler was a tough man.

"What brought you here?" Peter whispered.

"Thanks, Peter," she whispered back. "For a moment I was afraid you were going to start me on easy lessons in Irish. Davy introduced me to the irregular verbs all the way along the road."

"Don't blame him. The college authorities made the rule for this townland."

"Does everybody keep it?"

"Almost everybody."

"Dictatorship. What are we fighting a war for?"

"No. Quite within their rights. The place exists for a purpose. And the war doesn't bother them here."

"Peter, you've gone Gaelic."

"So have you. You're here too, aren't you?"

"Not to learn Irish."

"What for?"

"Holiday. At the River Hotel. They don't care what you speak over there."

"What brought you inside the college area?"

"Davy. I called to see how he was."

The clerical student from Armagh and the fair-haired teacher from Belfast crowded over the threshold, the two dogs barking at their heels. Peter glanced across the kitchen at Davy. Davy stared absently at Rita. Carson, once more with his back to the fire, called, out laughingly: "Did I hear a word of the tongue of the foreigner?"

Davy said: "I told her. But she would come."

Carson waggled a waggish finger: "Peter and Rita, you'll get the house a bad name. It'll be as bad as the year I took the girl from Johnny Peter's house to a ballroom dance in the River Hotel."

Hudie doubled with laughter: "The night, Jim boy, you tramped through Johnny Peter's young corn and knocked Johnny Peter himself into the cabbage garden."

The woman of the house took up the refrain:

"And the priest, God rest him, sitting here with a stick in his hand waiting for you. You were a young lad then."

"He told me I was worse than Dermott MacMurrough who brought in Strongbow and the Normans," said Carson with mock plaintiveness. The house rocked with laughter.

Peter knew she was awkward and embarrassed, not by Carson's laughing reprimand, but by the chance revelation of Davy's remark. She had made Davy bring her to Hudie's house. Peter hoped and was afraid to hope. He pitied her as he had not pitied her since the day her anger crumpled up and she sat with a white, wet face on the steps leading up to the band-platform in her own dancing-school. The teacher from Belfast began to play a mouth-organ. Peter took her hand. He whispered: "You can dance in any language." They went lightly up and down the floor between the hearth and the dresser. Carson grabbed the waist of the woman of the house and followed them. The girl placed the dinner-plates on the table, dodging in and out between the dancing couples. The two dogs barked with excitement. Hudie rattled out over the threshold. Davy returned to yesterday's *Irish Press*. Hudie chased the dogs out into the sunlight: sun on the rocks, the soft grass, the stone walls, on the red berries of the mountain ash, on the sand and the sea, on Errigal mountain, solid and regular like a monstrous pyramid raised by a monstrous people before the time of Milesius. The mouth-organ played. The dancing feet tapped up and down the floor. It was the land of the sun. The sun was in their veins.

III

After dinner, on Rita's invitation conveyed publicly through Peter, they set out walking to the River Hotel. They walked in single file up the narrow path between the rocks, short-cutting over one or two stone walls and around a triangular patch of potatoes to strike the main road at the post office. The post office was also a multiple shop. Further up the road were the school, another shop, a few big, slated houses, and the college. In front of the post office a dozen young men, and women, one or two priests, all visitors to the college, sat in the sun. The two parties joined, went noisily down the road past the white houses with their clumps of flowering fuchsia, gathering here and there another recruit until there were thirty of them marching in formation. A civil servant from Dublin marched in the lead, swinging a stick and leading the loud choruses. The women at the doors of the houses flapped their aprons and shouted, the children ran cheering, the dogs followed barking. Rita stayed close to Peter. He hoped and he was afraid to hope. She might be there because she wanted to be there, or her preference for his company might merely be the result of her fearful anxiety to avoid the more conscientious speakers of Gaelic. She walked well and easily, no swaying or swaggering, no crippling on feet accustomed to high heels and smooth pavements. The road was rough. She went along with a smooth springing walk. The rhythm of her step communicated itself to his own feet, to the beating of his heart, until he felt that her own heart was beating to the same rhythm. He was about to take her arm. Then he thought again that she was only protecting herself from the Gaelic speakers. So he joined noisily in the songs and tried to forget that she was there.

They left the main road, turning again towards the sea along a narrow, sandy path that was blessedly soft to the feet. They went down a slope with a lake on the left in a deep hollow of the rough, heathery hills. The path widened, crossed a bridge over the quick rock-tortured stream that twisted down from the lake to the long estuary. By a cottage on the slope above the bridge a small, tattered, gap-toothed man shouted imprecations at two rampaging cows. Another man, younger and more silent, stood at a gap in a stone wall, turning the heads of the cows down towards a spot of soft grazing at the edge of the stream. Carson scrambled to the top of the stone wall that fringed the path. He shouted:

"Mandy, a story for the strangers."

The small, tattered man approached them, waving a stick, shouting in welcome. The younger man followed. Peter sat by the edge of the path and watched them. Carson shouted over the stone wall into the partial deafness of the tattered man. The younger man looked over the wall, said nothing, appaised from under bushy red eyebrows the merits and demerits of the girls of the party. Peter could see the thoughts moving in the man's head, keeping time to the motion of the eyes, up and down, then swinging suddenly crossways to the next object of attraction. He found his own eyes moving in the same way, taking in print frocks, bare ankles, college blazers, neat costumes worn by young girls whose appearance told the world they were highly efficient primary- school teachers. Then his eyes met Rita's eyes. She sat exactly opposite him at the foot of the stone wall. His glance attracted her to cross the path and seat herself at his side.

"Enjoying yourself?" he whispered.

"What's it all about? Old Father Time over there having a bawling duet with Jim Carson."

"He's a story-teller. Jim wants him to perform, but he's shy before all the company.

"Public-house stories?"

"No, the genuine article. He's the nearest thing to Homer I've ever met in the flesh."

"God rest Homer. Who's the boy with the eye?"

"Did you notice it?"

"I feel it from here."

"He's a nephew."

The party was moving on again, ranks gapped and tattered, over the bridge, up a stiff slope, on a lane that twisted between high walls, and back again to the main road. The two men waved and shouted. She stood up wearily.

"Peter," she said, "all these people and their native tongue."

"Keep moving," said Davy, coming up behind them. "It's near teatime."

Davy was smiling, stiffly smiling. They kept moving, up the lane and along the high main road. Below them was the long estuary, the red sand, the sea whitening into surf around a dozen islands. They crossed a great bridge over a strong, wide river, saw the hotel ringed by trees, and between and beyond the trees they saw the mountains.

The walking, the shouting and singing, the salt bite of the great wind from the sea had sharpened their appetites. They crowded into the hotel dining-room, made themselves noisily at home, adjusted the tables to suit their needs. Davy worked himself into position with Rita on one side of him and Jim Carson on the other. Davy was determined. He still smiled stiffly, mechanically, when the atmosphere of the company seemed to call for smiling; but Peter knew there was no mirth behind that stupid, dogged determination. Davy had his teeth in something. He positively was not going to loosen his grip. He jettisoned his principles and spoke English to Rita. She laughed and answered and behaved very nicely to him. Peter could see it all. He told himself that he could understand it all. Then doubt returned on him like a mist and he understood nothing, absolutely nothing. God, it was maddening. He sat between the civil servant from Dublin and a young lady-teacher from Derry. She was a nice girl, plump-checked and sparkle-eyed, fair-haired, not too tall, springily corseted. He could feel her bounce against him every time she leaned close to hear what he was saying or to say something in return. She leaned close very frequently. It was difficult to hear anything above the babble of voices, the rattling of plates and knives and forks. The Dublin civil servant ate with an eloquent methodical silence.

Rita led the party to the ballroom, sat down at the piano and began to play. They danced. Davy stood near her, ostentatiously waiting his chance to whirl her from the keyboard, in and out among the active dancers. A stout, bespectacled man took her place and Davy had his chance. Peter, sitting in the corner of the room in a group that included the plump fair-headed teacher, studied the honest triumph on Davy's face. And Rita seemed to be enjoying herself. His doubt became bitter, depressing certainty, blasting and blackening the brief exultation of the sunny morning. Even the sunshine was withering. The ballroom window opened on flower-beds and a green lawn, on hedges and trees and the white road visible through the branches. The birds and the bees were silent. The flowers drooped in the weary, shaded heat. The noise of the river came up to them with a sultry, menacing loudness.

Anyway, he couldn't lower himself to race against Davy in the Rita Keenan stakes. Two brothers going neck and neck for one girl. It was unseemly. Even if he got there first, there might be no cheers for him at the winning-post, no welcoming smile from the prize, from the fair lady for whose smile the knights contended. God, he was getting his periods mixed, tiny cotton jockeys, massive iron knights. There were more fish in the sea. More mixed metaphors, as dizzying as mixed drinks. The sea was all around him, dancing up and down the floor, at least fifteen passable young women and not more than two or three particularly and steadily attached. He let his eyes wander like the eyes of the nephew of Mandy the story-teller glinting over the stone wall. There was the fair-headed teacher. He couldn't help seeing her. He suspected that she had deliberately placed her plump, attractive person between himself and the light. He asked her to dance.

Rita was back at the piano. He felt her eyes upon him when he led his new capture to the floor. He didn't look around.

"This is your first time here," said the fair-headed fish.

"Yes. I was never at the college before."

"Talk English if you like."

"What about the college rule?"

"I don't give a damn. My own Irish isn't so hot. But what can you do when you're a teacher?"

"I suppose it is useful."

"Not so much in the Six Counties. Still, the priests like it and the priests manage the schools."

"But what about the patriotic motive, Miss —?"

"Harrison. May Harrison. Patriotism? That's all very well if you can afford it. We have to live. It suits literary people like yourself.

Gives them something to write about."

"Who told you I was literary?"

"My brother Tom. We've heard a lot about you at home."

They locked arms for the swing. She bounced against him like a warm ball of india-rubber. In the thick of the dance, speech ceased to be possible. He remembered Tom Harrison, a good student due for ordination in twelve months' time. Dowdall had always found it very difficult to be charitable to Tom, but then Dowdall had active and unexplainable likes and dislikes. Tom was a simple soul and Dowdall was complex enough to envy, even detest, simplicity. Tom was like his sister, round, cheery, guileless, bouncing rather than living from one day to the next. Perhaps, on second thoughts, Tom was even more guileless than his sister. Girls had their own mysterious ways of gathering wisdom, their own methods of masking it in coyness or clingingness or vestal independence or in the other thing that cinema-bills named glamour.

They sat beside each other near the wide-open window, smelt the flowers, heard the sullen noise of the river, slowly recovered their breath.

She said: "I always wanted to meet you. I heard so much about you."

For a transient moment he was flattered. She went on: "I read some of your poems too. In the college magazines that Tom used to bring home at Christmas."

He blushed, then apologised for the redness of his face and blamed the heat of the day.

"It is warm," she said. "How can they keep dancing in this stifling room? It must be lovely beside the river or down by the sea."

"Like a walk?"

They slipped out by the open french window, around the corner of the hotel under a glass balcony that compressed the heat into grey visibility, across a flat lawn, down a cart-track that led directly to the river. The water came down leaping over the rocks, bursting into foam the colour of froth on porter, growing steady and strong and smooth before it plunged hollowly into a deep pool between walls of high rock. The track followed the river away from the hotel, the two shops, the church and the cluster of houses at the crossroads. They walked hand in hand. She talked steadily, raising her voice to make herself heard above the noise of the water around the rocks.

She was in the best of good humour, dancing from foot to foot with a lightness that belonged to a slimmer waist and a more delicate figure. She was an athletic girl, played hockey and tennis, rowed, went on long walks and cycle trips with other members of youth holiday organisations. They slept in hostels governed by certain regulations. They made their own meals. It was healthy. It was economic. You saw the country.

Peter led her away from the river, across a field, over a ditch, through a gapped grey wall into the ruins of the old coastguard station. The grey stones were hot to the touch. In the deserted parade-ground the tattered weeds and nettles drooped with dry weariness. Half a dozen cattle stood quietly in the shadow of the wall. Down below, the river curved through a few green fields founded on the mud carried down from the flat bogland at the foot of the mountains. They saw a little harbour with a factory, a store, a few lifeless boats beached under the shadow of a high rock. Beyond the rock a chain of islands faded westwards into the Atlantic. Grey ruined walls, vanished coastguards, vanished smugglers and makers of poteen, a factory and a timber store that meant that one man of the people had risen in the world to own shops and lorries, to give employment and wages. Guerrilla war had burst in on those old walls, smashed the gates, emptied the rooms, burned anything that would burn, left the place to the weeds and the cattle.

"I like the open-air life," she said. "But I adore books and pictures and the theatre. Much more than dancing."

He looked at the dull, hot sky reflecting itself in the lazy sea, and wondered when the rain would come. They sat on the grass some distance from the wall. She lighted a cigarette and blew rings meditatively. Their shoulders touched.

"Do you smoke, Peter?"

"I do. Too hot to-day, though."

"It is hot."

"I like books too," he said lamely.

"That goes without saying. My brother showed me something you wrote once in college. I wish I could write like that. Wouldn't have much trouble with English exams."

He winced, recovered himself, put his arm around her shoulder.

"What do you read mostly?" he asked.

"All sorts of stuff. Poetry mostly. James Elroy Flecker."

He said: "I have seen old ships sail like swans asleep."

"Yes. I know that one. Do say it, Peter."

"Too hot."

She pitched her cigarette-butt away from him. It burned out in wispy, blue smoke. He pressed her shoulders tightly, tilted up her chin with his right hand.

"Do you mind, May?"

"Do you think should you? After all, I know you only for an hour or so."

He looked at his watch. "Fifty-five minutes to be exact." She laughed and said:

"Still, I suppose it's all right. I feel as though we were rocked in the same cradle." She kept on laughing. "Tom told me so much about you. I had imagined you before I saw you."

"What was I like?"

"Not half as nice as you are."

He kissed her. Her lips bounced off his with a futile touch that had in it certainly no mingling of souls, no fusion of spirit with spirit. The old worn phrases rolled over in his mind like the ironic comment of a tumbling clown. He thought again of india-rubber. May Harrison and the mingling of souls didn't belong in the same mental sequence. She had a soul. A soul to save, precious and immortal in the eyes of God. She was a good girl, sincere, earnest, a little guileless like her brother, but not with the guilelessness that didn't know how to defend itself. Otherwise she was a rubberoid sphere bouncing from one day to the next, one year to the next, from the cradle to the grave, bouncing with aim now and again at the head or the heart of a man. Some day she would hit the target and find happiness. But not to-day. Not to-day.

He thought uneasily of the dance still going on in the hotel. Maybe the dancers had found the heat too much for them, had retreated to the lawn to sit and sip cool drinks. Rita would wonder where he had gone. Davy would wonder. What difference did it make? Davy would rejoice. He didn't know what Rita would do. At least she wouldn't bounce. She had a soul, to save or lose, a spirit that informed every action of her body. He could not escape from her this way. As far as he was concerned she had become part of this grey land of rock, tall walls, tiny fields, just as years ago she had belonged to the sun on the streets, the blue whirring wings of the pigeons, the tall spires, the river, the blue circle of hills. But when he tried to see her as she had been that morning in Hudie's house, he had only a vague recollection of neat, stockingless ankles, a white dress. She was beautiful. He wondered why he had never realised that before. He could not see her face clearly. It dissolved backwards into the thunderous rush of black water bursting over rocks, carrying brown froth down to the placid harbour, to the infinite laziness of the sea. So he didn't know whether she smiled or frowned.

"I'll see you again, Peter," said May.

He didn't attempt to kiss her again, or even to hold her hand as they made their way back to the hotel. She was a good girl. She didn't expect any elaborate demonstrations. They would have shocked her coming from the author of those piodious poems in the college annual. When he thought of them he could feel his soul cringe. Then he laughed at his own vanity.

"What's the joke, Peter?"

"Nothing. That is, something I remembered. You'll be on the excursion?"

"Yes, certainly. I love the boats."

Through the green hedge they saw the party sitting in groups on the lawn. They circled the lawn, hidden by the hedge, slipped in through a side-gate and a side-door, out on to the lawn down the wide circling steps from the front door of the hotel. Rita and Davy sat together on a white garden seat. There was no singing, no noise, and the quiet evening coming down from the high places. Far away a long roll of thunder went across the low sky.

"Welcome back," Carson said.

A thin, red-headed girl looked up at the sky and shivered. She said: "We'll be soaked on the way home"

"Cheer up, Greta," Carson said. "We'll have supper first." Somebody shouted: "Food." The party moved like one man towards the door of the hotel. Peter found himself walking up the steps with Rita.

"Having a good time, Rita?" he said. She didn't answer. They crowded into the dining-room. Davy sat beside her again. Again the sky rumbled with thunder, dim and far away, moving behind the wall of the mountains.

IV

Davy had seldom felt in such particularly good form. He was free from the house by the lake, from the constant fear of detection, the morose reminder of what human beings could sink to, that came to him every time he looked at Lanty; free from the constant, irritating dominance of Dick Slevin. Davy was afraid of Slevin. It was not physical fear. It was no sense of moral inferiority. It was something remotely resembling second sight. In some obscure way he felt that Dick Slevin, his quick, neat movements, the smile going side ways off his face, stood for evil and ill luck. Davy didn't think himself a bit better than Dick Slevin. Davy was no pharisee. Poor Dick had been unfortunate right from the word "Go." Look even at his schoolboy escapades that at some stage or other went wrong like the smile going away and slipping off the side of his face. Once it was a head smashed accidentally through a closed window. Once it was a whirling fall from a tree that ended with serious concussion and a month in hospital. A hundred boys could fall a hundred times while playing football on the old field above the convent. But when Dick fell it had to be precisely on the spot where a fragment of iron piping came up rusty and jagged out of the ground. People could get superstitious about men like that and women like that. They would say a hard fate followed them, or God preserve us from a hard fate, or they never had luck and they never brought luck. Davy was frightened by that last reflection. He knew that the whole idea seemed stupid, pagan as the belief in jealous gods that were angry when men prospered. It wasn't Slevin's fault. All the poor fellow needed was some sympathy and what the Yankees called an even break. But somehow Dick Slevin never did seem to get the even break, and words of sympathy weren't worth their weight in wind. The fellow was difficult to live with. God, he was difficult, with his gun and his "Catch me, I'm John Dillinger." Once upon a time you could keep saying that all this was for Ireland. But the confinement and close contact in a smoky hut rubbed the gilt off that sentiment. Poor Dick didn't give a damn about Ireland or about any other country between Borneo and the Baltic. He didn't square off with anything Davy had heard or read of Pearse in Arbour Hill, MacWiney in Brixton, Casement in the Old Bailey. Davy was glad to be rid of Slevin.

His rude good-humour returned. His arrogance returned. He triumphed even over the way he felt about Rita Keenan, enough to suspect the motive behind her earnest wish to visit Hudie's house. He was afraid of Peter, not as he was afraid of Slevin. Peter could flatten him in a rough-and-tumble. Peter had somewhere in his character a solidity and a hardness that did not need the Dutch courage of arrogance or rude good-humour. Yet the ebullient effect of relief from restraint swept Davy onwards to push himself into the place that he knew quite well Peter wanted to occupy. Sure enough Davy was in love with Rita Keenan. He had been that way for longer than he could remember. But when he walked deliberately across Peter's path there was as much devilment as love underneath his waistcoat, as much desire to show that Davy Quinn was as good a man as the next.

The salt wind of these places had filled uproariously into his lungs. The pulse of the sparse earth, stretched like fruitful, pliable metal around the grey rocks, had beaten upwards into his blood. It was a great life. Early every morning he tumbled actively out of bed, ate a healthy breakfast cooked by the woman of the house, went out with the man of the house to labour the rich little fields gathered in a green cluster in the shelter of the mountains. The farm was large for that part of the country. The land was free from rocks and exceptionally fruitful, well managed and well stocked, displaying in clean outhouses, solidly built walls, clear free-running drains, what two industrious generations could do, working with some natural advantages in their favour. It was more than a hiding-place—it was a home. The house was whitewashed, spotlessly clean. The bed he slept in smelt of cool, chaste cleanliness. The woman was kind, volubly sympathetic. Her husband was kind, gruffly sympathetic. They had known Davy for some years and very gladly offered him what refuge their home afforded until better times returned, until he could move back into the towns and find a job for himself. Fortunately he wasn't important enough or notorious enough to have the police on his tail on both sides of the border. Slevin was the man they wanted; and a few weeks of normal life had so utterly detached him from Slevin that he could hardly believe he had ever lived in the hovel by the lake, or raced in terror across the one street of Ballyclogher.

A man he knew in a little town a few miles up the coast was

opening a factory for the manufacture of cheap toys. There was an opening for Davy, the prospect of regular work, very little risk, the pleasant company of forty or fifty girls, dark-haired and white-haired. In that corner of the country the girls were either decidedly blonde or decidedly brunette, with perhaps an occasional redhead. The prospect was pleasant enough.

Not that he was forgetting about Rita. He did love her, even if she was a strange class of a girl. Swinging a scythe on a hill behind the house he had watched her wheel her bicycle up the narrow path from the road that ran between the mountains and the sea. He couldn't be mistaken: the strong, neat ankles; the white summer frock fitting lightly to the lines of her body; the well- shaped face; the abundant black hair. Somehow the clothes girls wore in the summertime gave them a new life, a vigorous, vital beauty; brought out something in a man that had been fearfully concealed during the cold days, the dark days. She was beautiful. The realisation of that beauty weakened and frightened him. The beauty of the sea, the grey land, the high mountains was a safe sort of beauty. It went over a man like a smooth, warm wave. It brought him peace. But the mark of beauty on another human face or the lines of beauty in another human body only made him conscious of the fragility of beauty, of his own perilous weakness. Davy could not define what he felt when he watched her walk towards them up the path. He felt ill and dizzy. She was beautiful. She had promised to marry him. He loved her.

He scrambled over the stone wall and ran to meet her. What he meant to do was to put his arms around her there and then and kiss her. But her half-smile and the slow, firm handshake somehow or other punctured his cocksureness. You never knew when you had her.

"Hello Rita, " he said. " What are you doing here?"

"Aren't you glad to see me?"

"Of course I'm glad. But I never expected you. It's a surprise. I haven't seen you since the night the people were out in the old quarry. It's good to see you again."

She wanted to tell him something. She had come all the way from the hotel to tell him something, but faced suddenly by his cocksure good-nature she couldn't find any words. He wheeled her bicycle up the path to the long, white farmhouse, and they went in out of the sun. The kitchen was clean and cool, a scrubbed white table and chairs to match it, plates shining on a white dresser, a long-tailed clock on one wall, a picture of Robert Emmet above the mantelpiece, a local grocer's calendar with a picture of the Magi and a huge star shining in a sky of impossible blue. In the patch of flowers before the door the black bees worked musically.

"This is heaven," she said.

"It is now."

She didn't even smile. She asked him where the people of the house were. Then she sat down on a chair beside the table and rested her elbows wearily on the shining wood. She was tired with the labour of walking and pushing up the road from the hotel, tired with the heat of the sun and the great wind persistently tangling her hair before her eyes, tired with the reaction that followed the utter collapse of her resolution. For two days she had made up her mind, strengthened and stabilised her will. Then at the critical moment she failed, she couldn't do it. She felt Davy's arm around her shoulder. It didn't matter, anyway. She couldn't do a damn thing about it.

"We could be very happy in a place like this," Davy was saying. "Just the two of us."

She didn't dispute the point. She said: "It is very nice."

"Nice? It's glorious. This is freedom, Rita. The sort of freedom that the people in towns never hear about."

"The towns aren't so bad in their own way."

It was a cautionary remark, but Davy wasn't paying any attention to red lights. His arm tightened around her shoulders. He went lyrical about it all; the house, the land, the wind, the sea, the mountains. There was something genuinely infectious about his enthusiasm if she had been in the mood. When he came close enough to kiss her she turned away her face to look suddenly out of the window. She said:

"Davy, don't you hear footsteps?"

He said innocently that was impossible, but he went to the door and out into the sunshine and looked around. When he came back she was on her feet, wary in spite of her weariness. With her back towards him she said:

"Do you ever go over to see the folk at the college?"

"Sometimes. I was thinking of going to-day. If it doesn't rain."

She walked to the door, looked critically at the spotlessly blue sky. "Not a chance. It won't rain. Take me with you, Davy. I'd love to go only the rule about Gaelic gives me the jitters."

His cocksure, good-natured innocence bent a little under the strain. She found it a wearisome journey. Davy had no bicycle. They walked to the hotel, rested and refreshed themselves with lunch. The tide was out and they short-cutted straight across the flat sand of the estuary, wading in one or two places, balancing perilously on slippery stepping-stones where the river that came down in tumult over the rocks near Mandy's house widened out placidly over the sand. They could see the college before them high on a headland that rose higher as they approached it until they were walking in its shadow, following the path the sand-eel diggers had followed at the last ebb. Davy was persistently informative, childishly proud of his knowledge of the place and the people, the habits of the people, the language of the people that should be the language spoken all over the country. He began to talk in that language. She wearied her mind in efforts to unearth fragments buried there since the day she had left secondary school. She wasn't very successful. He began to teach her, gently, patiently, with solid, unshakable good-nature. She knew it was all very true. She admired his enthusiasm, his quite obvious purity of motive. But she didn't give a damn about the whole business, didn't care if the people spoke Yiddish or Esperanto.

Going up the slope to Hudie's house she knew she had been bored as she had never been bored in her whole life. Her resolution returned. She stiffened and strengthened it. He was good. God, he was good, honest, everything a man should be. But the whole thing wasn't possible, feasible, sensible. It never had been sensible. It never would be sensible. She was amazed and a little ashamed at her own sense of relief when Peter came down from the bedroom, sat beside her, spoke to her in English, danced with her on the concrete floor. She put her soul into the dance. That was one way of telling Davy the truth. She tried to make it obvious. It would be better for everybody that way.

It wasn't going to be as easy as all that. That night at the quarry a deep, destructive feeling of pity, a sense of loyalty to a lost cause, had kept her standing by Davy and resisting Peter. But it would have been much easier then to have told Davy that she didn't belong to his world by any law of God, man, Mother Nature or Mother Ireland. That night he would have taken it humbly. Now he walked in the sun and the great wind, around the stiff arrogance of the grey rocks, bouncing on the miserly pride that the sparse soil had in its own existence. When she danced with Peter, Davy sullenly held the *Irish Press*, reading the Gaelic column on page two, as a symbol of passive resistance. At the post office he paired off with an active young woman who belonged to one of the new Gaelic organisations in Dublin. They marched on the streets with banners that asked the people to speak Irish, ordered the Government to order the people to speak Irish, ordered the Government to do a whole lot of things that the young Gael would never have heard of if it hadn't been for the Government. They spoke off dray-carts at street corners to an audience that usually consisted of their own members, two bored and duty-bound Civic Guards, a few casual listeners, a score of children. They showed films in the streets; they organised Gaelic festivals in public parks, interested themselves in the development of an Irish cinema industry that had no existence; talked about the land, the decay of rural life, about forestry, fisheries, parish councils, mineral wealth, factories, the rights of labour, the chains that bound the banks to British sterling, the pressing need of monetary reform, the question of Partition. They were young and vigorous. They had a great deal of self- confidence and a great deal of hope. Davy belonged there and she was content to let him stay where he belonged.

But Davy was not content. Passive resistance changed into active attack, ostentatiously pushing in between Peter and herself when they were struggling to find the fragile thing that had broken long ago when Peter put on a suit of black clothes, turned away from the long, sunny evenings and the pigeons going in blue circles around the humpy roofs. It was very hard to be angry with Davy. He had his reasons. He would be able to produce justifying arguments. It was much easier to be angry with Peter; to feel irritation against him increase when he fell back before Davy's boisterous charge; to feel cold and weak and horribly sick when he was gone from the ballroom in the company of that fair-headed girl; to pass him on the way into supper and casually leave his greeting unanswered. She wanted to hurt him. She wanted to protect herself from a surrender that made her legs non-existent and her body like water. Back in the dining-room she hated his steady, hard-chinned quietness. She wanted to burst in on it with some physical contact, like the shout an explorer might utter in some lost valley where no other man had ever walked. The shout would go off into an infinity of echo answering echo, rock replying to rock, tree whispering to tree, making immortal the cry of one human voice, the triumph of achievement in one human heart.

But around her was the babel of thirty insignificant voices, the tap-tapping of trivial table utensils. In her ear was the commonplace voice of honest Davy. He spoke to her in English, spoke in Irish to the girl from Dublin who sat at his left hand. He introduced them to each other and the girl answered Rita's greeting in English that had a decided flavour of Tipperary, then spoke again in Irish to Davy who answered in Irish, translated into English for Rita's benefit, shouted something in Irish to Jim Carson who sat opposite them. She knew that Carson understood the situation, was almost prepared for the sepulchral voice replying solemnly in Latin that smelt of the bog. The table rocked with laughter. Thank God for Jim Carson.

V

Peter left the dining-room and went upstairs looking for the gents'. A few men of the party had found their way to the bar, heating up the engines for the return journey. He heard Carson's voice solemnly laying down the law for the benefit of a commercial traveller from Dublin and an inspector from the Department of Education. A school-teacher from Belfast raised a tentative Presbyterian voice, was promptly shouted down by the dictatorial Carson. Jim was enjoying himself.

Beyond the bathroom door a french window opened on iron steps that curved down gracefully to the lawn. Peter opened the window and stood at the head of the steps, crushed and oppressed with the dark warmth of the dusk, listening to the faint, distant rumblings, as if the sky held within itself a monotonously rebellious life. Down below the party girded their loins for the walk back to the college. Hard heels tapped along the tiled corridor to the ladies' cloakroom. Somebody tinkled wearily at the ballroom piano. A girl laughed loudly in the kitchen. The sounds were casual, feeble, ephemeral like the voices of ghosts. They sparkled suddenly into existence, were caught up in the noise of the river, swept recklessly along into the long murmur of the sea.

He knew that he must do something, that he could not mingle with the party, take his place with May Harrison, walk back to the college and leave Rita alone in the hotel. Davy would go back with Carson, and Davy would walk every inch of the way with an elation that spoke of something attempted and something done. Peter couldn't bear to think of it. Behind him footsteps were coming up the stairs and along the corridor. He went down the iron stairs in a few whirling, perilous leaps, crouched for a moment breathlessly in the shadow of the wall, dodged around the corner to the rear of the hotel. Through a lighted window he saw a girl washing dishes. He tapped and she opened the window, leaned out a round, pretty face and strong, firm shoulders.

She said: "Looking for something?"

"Maybe I was looking for you."

"Not on your life. I've seen dozens like you in England."

"Did you work there?"

"Two years. My mother died. I had to come home. Awful dump, this."

"It could be worse."

"Everything could be worse."

She viewed him with easy good-humour. The steam from the dishwater pillared upwards around her face and neck. She might have been a placid, benevolent enchantress brewing blessings for good children. She said:

"I'll have to close the window or the water will get cold. Never saw as much grease as there is in this place. Besides, if the mistress comes around I'm as good as sacked."

"Wait a minute."

"What do you want? You're not boozed. Did you lose your way?"

"Can I get down to the river this way?"

"You can. Want to drown yourself? Right through the wee black gate."

"I'm dodging the party."

"Don't blame you. They're a noisy gang. Still, they seem to have a good time."

"Do you know Miss Keenan?"

"You bet. The good-looking dame. She's decent. And what a figure. If I was a man . . ."

“Would you ever tell her. . . .?”

“That you’ve gone that way. I will, sir. Anything to oblige.”

He reached over the sill, placed the tip in her warm, wet hand. She thanked him, blew a dishwatery kiss after him as he went through the black gate, across a rutted garden, down the path to the river. The shadows swallowed him. The shadows swallowed the hotel until the casual, tinkling noises died as if muffled in a blanket, and his ears were throbbing to the crash and the swirl of water going down over the rocks and around the rocks, gushing with compressed violence between the rocks, conquering and covering the rocks, being conquered and broken into reckless white spray by the rocks. Stiff rocks; and strong water rushing to the infinite sea. The whole secret of life was there, symbolised, allegorised: the force, the incredible haste, the damaging, shattering obstacles, the infinite blue peace.

He sat near the edge of the water. He waited for the sound of her feet coming down the stony path from the black gate, for the flash of her white dress in the intricate shadows, for the smooth firmness of her voice. He waited for something else that he was afraid to define. His muscles ached with an impatience that went deeper and further than his body. Then suddenly he heard the sound of footsteps, not two feet on the path, but sixty feet on the hard road advancing towards the bridge. They marched jauntily in step. They sang: “Left, right, left, right—Steady, boys, and step together.” They stepped together. He saw them against the last line of light as they went two-deep over the high bridge. For a moment their loud singing challenged the cry of the water. Then they were gone out of sight and hearing, steadily stepping together under the low, hot sky. The sound of their feet went back through the centuries to the sea-rovers working in unison to haul their boats zig-zagging upwards out of reach of the tide. The sound of their feet went out over the whole world, Germany, Britain, France, Poland, Italy, Finland, Russia, Japan, marching and singing songs to the sound of their own feet. *Steady, boys, and step together*. The rhythm of the words hammered into his brain, mingled with the rhythm of the river and the slow monotonous wash of the sea, until waiting became an agony that he could bear no longer. She wasn’t coming. He was on his feet again, dazed and bewildered, when he heard the rattle of stones, the movement of two feet coming down the path.

It was the round-faced cheerful queen of the steaming dishwater. She passed along the path within a few yards of the place where he stood, turned with the path to go upwards against the course of the river. He shouted after her. She halted, looked over her shoulder, said "Good night."

He said: "Did you deliver my message?"

"Yes, sir."

"Any answer?"

"Miss Keenan didn't give me an answer."

"Did she say anything?"

"Nothing at all. I think, sir, she's gone to her bed."

"Gone to her bed ?"

There was an awkward pause. Below them the water thundered down with a dull, metallic resonance.

"You take a dangerous place for your walk," he said. "Or maybe you're thinking of going over the edge."

"I'm not going for a walk. I've while off. My sister lives over there. There's a footbridge."

She waved her hand vaguely at the darkness beyond the river, then moved away from him along the path.

"Give your sister my best wishes."

She waved a hand, called back at him as she went: "Begging your pardon, mister. You'll catch nothing there but your death of cold. There's more heat in the lounge."

When she had gone into the darkness he took her advice and went up the path to the hotel, around the corner of the building, up the wide steps to a balcony that opened off the lounge. He found a seat in a shady corner where he could see in through a half-opened french window, and across the carpeted floor to the wide curving stairway. A few people sat here and there in silent, perspiring groups, too uncomfortably hot for sleep, too suspicious of the low sky and the faint growlings of thunder to risk themselves in the open air. Inside the window three men clinked glasses and talked. His eyes examined the room, went as far as they could up the stairway. Inside the window the commercial traveller from Dublin said:

"That Carson fellow knew what he was talking about. You can't beat those Six County fellows on all this business of Partition. They're full of it up to the ears."

The departmental inspector said: "I suppose it's because they live there. Strikes me Catholics and Protestants are all alike over there. One as bad as the other."

"He didn't offer any solution," said the Presbyterian teacher, "beyond saying that the British Army should withdraw. My own solution is . . ."

A faint roll of thunder cut through the middle of the solution. A breath of wind went round the lawn and round the green hedge like a living whisper. God was good to Carson and to that trio of congenital idiots inside the window. Get yourself a good, big, general problem like the social advance of mankind, unemployment, poverty, international relations, or the more confined political middens of your own country. Don't, for God's sake, ever get near enough to that generalisation to risk turning it into a personal issue. That was what Davy did. If you must think of love then think of it like a court poet, a thing of stately attitudes and balanced lines. Avoid the horror of the moment when the soul is negligible and the body a dry furnace, when the eyes go over the soft carpet of a hotel lounge like the eyes of a sun-maddened, thirst-maddened wanderer searching the red sand for green leaves and cool water.

"And what *is* your solution, Mr. MacPherson?"

"Well, you must take into account innumerable problems that are passed over in the conventional opinions of nationalists. For instance, Dublin cannot have legalised contraceptive clinics. Then the bias of the Catholic Church against modern divorce law is notorious . . ."

The thin Presbyterian voice went on and on, each phrase building up in Peter's mind a picture of the soul of the man. He might be any one of a dozen different types of Ulster Unionist or Ulster Protestant. Even as he tried to place the man in a category Peter realised wearily the inadequacy of the political terminology of his country. To say that a man, living in Ireland, near the close of the first half of the twentieth century, was a Unionist might mean anything or nothing. Could any man now want a return to the shade of bribery-and-corruption Castlereagh, to one Parliament for the two islands? That was Unionism. Now, there was one Dublin government controlling twenty-six counties, one Belfast government controlling six counties, and in between a line of separation known as the Border. Any dozen men would have a dozen possible solutions for that problem of division and disunion, or perhaps a dozen possible reasons to show why the problem should not be solved. The crank creaking inside the window had the thirteenth solution, abandoning the morals both of his Presbyterian predecessors and his Catholic neighbours, to find in the end only another foundation for the awful thing that Cain and Abel had discovered in the beginning of all time. Men would never be at a loss for something to differ about. That was the voice of a man who would go to war in defence of chemical appliances and bonds that did not bind.

The voice said:

"The Catholics of the Six Counties will have to stop talking about persecution. Everything that has happened to them, they brought on themselves. They refused to co-operate in the new state."

The commercial traveller said: "Co-operate my foot. They never had a chance to co-operate. Even Lloyd George knew in 1920 that the only cement that would build the state was constant coercion. Do you deny the facts of political jerrymander, discrimination in the giving of jobs? What do you make of the Belfast pogrom in 1935?"

"I should say an attempt at mass sterilisation," said the inspector, and the debate dissolved into barroom laughter. It was one way of ending an argument, thought Peter. You laughed and you solved nothing. The other way was to end it in a fight that, in the long run, also solved nothing. The laughter was preferable. It cracked no skulls, broke no bones, left no bitter feelings. It was the sweet Shakespearean antidote for minds diseased. If for five minutes only he could stand apart from his own personal puzzle and see it in the light of laughter, he was saved. Think of it. Love. The foundations on which love built its dwelling. The flower with its roots in the midden. The painful cry in the body, so easily satisfied—the cry in the soul that was never satisfied. He tried to toss it backwards from him, to see laughter glimmer out of it like light from the stones of a valuable ring. Then the commercial traveller said: "Some dame. She has poise." The inspector said: "Why do we have to grow old?" The apostle of sterility had no comment to make.

She came down the stairs and across the lounge towards the door. He waited in a sort of paralysis, his heart pounding like the beat of a hammer, until she should go walking down the steps. He waited and waited. She did not appear. Swivelling round where he sat he watched her go back again across the lounge and slowly ascend the stairs. He followed her, walking with a deliberation that cost him tremendous effort, wondering would the commercial man and the inspector notice anything peculiar, insanely fearing that they would whistle impudently to the rhythm of his feet. With her hand on the knob of her bedroom door she saw him approach, turned to face him.

"Peter, what are you doing here?"

"When the mountain wouldn't come to Mahomet . . ."

"What did you expect me to do? Take a message straight from the kitchen"

"I hadn't any other way of sending a message."

"You could have mentioned it to me."

"Before the whole assembly? Before Davy?"

"This shyness doesn't become you. Miss Harrison must have put the fear of God into you."

He thought for a moment, steadying himself with one shoulder against the polished doorpost. He must be careful, discreetly and delicately careful, or the whole situation would go up in hot, scalding steam. It might be just a lovers' quarrel. On the other hand it might be the sort of argument that ended in a fight, with nothing solved and bones broken on both sides. He struggled to smile.

"Look, Rita. This is foolish. It's cheap. We shouldn't be going on like this. We were all right in the morning if it hadn't been for Davy."

"And Miss Harrison."

"Leave her out of it. It's cheap to go on like this."

"I know it's cheap. The whole thing's cheap. Catching a half-witted flapper when she dives at your head is as cheap as anything I know."

"Rita. What's come over us? It was all right this morning, wasn't it? When you came into Hudie's kitchen. I knew it was all right then. The way we danced together. The way it was years ago before I ever left home. We had to get away from that town. There's ill luck about it. We'll have to get away from it for ever. We can make our own life somewhere else. In Dublin, or across in England."

She stood with her back to the door, very white in her white dress, against the dark wood. She said:

"Peter, what are you talking about?"

" Us, Rita. You and me."

"There isn't any us, Peter. I gave my word."

"I gave mine. I broke it."

" Oh, go home, Peter. Leave me alone. What will the people here think? Go back to Hudie's house, go anywhere. Leave me alone."

He reached forward and gripped her by the shoulder, tightening his fingers until she stiffened with pain, leading her with him to the window that opened to the iron stairway. She didn't move, didn't speak or protest when he kissed her, with no passion, with cold anger. He loosened his grip, stepped out on to the staircase. He said:

"You can have Davy now. He can have you. You keep your word to him. He'll keep his word to Mother Ireland. I broke my word to the God that made me, and you, and Davy. As far as I know I broke it because of you. I don't blame you. Don't blame yourself. Be happy with Davy."

He went down the staircase, across the soft lawn, down the road towards the great bridge. Halfway across she overtook him, ran with a cry into his arms. The grey stone of the parapet was rough and cold against their bodies. The tormented water was tossed beneath the arches, crying as the girl had cried feeling the sharp force of something stronger even than the desire of the river for the sea.

VI

Going up the hill from the bridge, the dark sky above him was suddenly split open. Tall rocks and stone walls leaped out at him, leaped backwards into the darkness and vanished before the rumble and roll of thunder. A sensible man would go back to the hotel. But then he was no longer a sensible man. He was a spirit, a power of the night and the darkness, a brother to the tumult of thunder and the radiance of lightning. He went forward, drunk with elation and power, inspired with a vision of things placed at last in their proper order, of the world remade and rearranged.

He counted the long brattles of thunder, seven between the schoolhouse at the first corner and the zinc-roofed shop on the hill where the lane went down between stone walls to the bridge at Mandy's house. Seven times the noise began back somewhere in the mountains, came down the valley, growling and crackling over his head. Seven times the lightning flashed, showing every field and stone and white house in a radiant intimacy. Once looking back over his shoulder he saw the skeleton of the coastguard station, very black against the white light. May Harrison, and "I read your poems in the college annual," and the india-rubber kiss bouncing flippantly into nothingness. Dead and gone now, swept away by that ecstasy at the bridge, the feeling of cold, rough stone, the cry of the water surrendering itself to the pull of the sea.

In the hot, breathless silence that followed the seventh flash, the rain began. He heard the first drops on the tin roof of the roadside shop and then, going down the twists of the lane towards the bridge, he was quite suddenly walking in water. Water squelched in his shoes, soaked through his jacket and shirt, tightened his trousers around his legs until movement was a dismal, flapping, sodden agony. Far out over the sea an eighth brattle of thunder sounded derisive mockery of all mortal elation. He defied it. He sang and whistled his way down the lane, splashing hilariously in water that overflowed from the choked drains at the bottom of the stone walls. Leaning on the parapet of the bridge he shouted poetry at the swelling waters. "*Blow, winds, and crack your cheeks!*" From his saturated shirt rivulets went racing down his back. "*You cataracts and hurricanoes, spout.*" The contrast between the spouting cataracts and the rivulets racing down his lumbar spine amused him. He threw back his head and laughed upwards into the lacing rain, then stopped to wonder had he taken leave of his senses. Still, the mood had not deserted him when he hammered on the door of Mandy's house, threw his weight against it as it tardily and reluctantly opened, stepped quickly over the threshold. The words running from his mind to his lips were about poor, naked wretches in the pitiless storm, their houseless heads and unfed sides, their looped and windowed raggedness. He might have declaimed the lines to Mandy or to Mandy's nephew, the man with the wandering eye. But the declamatory lust perished in a kitchen crowded to the door, where Jim Carson, standing with his back to the red hearth, raised his right hand and shouted: "Three cheers, ladies and gentlemen, for the prodigal son, for the one that was lost and is found." They cheered frantically. The water gathered in a pool around his limp shoes. Davy sat on a brown meal-chest near the one window. Davy didn't cheer. May Harrison turned from trimming the wick of the oil-lamp. She didn't cheer, but she smiled an amiable welcome. She didn't know anything and she wasn't the sort that bothered guessing about what she wouldn't want to know.

You're soaked to the skin," she said. "Mandy, have you a spare suit in the house?"

On his seat in the corner Mandy looked blankly at his own clothes, as varied as a tattered patchwork quilt.

"One suit for every day in the week," he said. "The same suit." He slapped his left palm on his left knee, laughed through gapped teeth, spat hilariously into the hot yellow ashes. Mandy's nephew helped Peter out of his soaking jacket, proffered the loan of a tailed coat that dangled dismally behind the door, a relic of respectable walking at respectable funerals back in the days of the Land League and the Irish Parliamentary Party. A man in the kitchen had, surprisingly, a pair of shorts and a football jersey. Somebody else produced a pair of white sand-shoes. Seated on the outshot bed, with the curtains modestly drawn, Peter stripped and reattired himself, passed the wet clothes to Carson, who squeezed the water out of them at the sink and draped them along the brace above the heat of the fire. Carson did all this with demonstrative good humour, gestured for the audience, feigned attempts to push through the curtain the girls who sat nearest to the bed; with words that were mockingly serious, advising Peter to a proper modesty in dress and deportment. Carson didn't need to trouble himself guessing. He saw Davy sitting silently on the meal-chest. He saw Peter and himself, knee-deep in the grass on the railway bank, shouting warning to two uniformed school-girls running helplessly for the train. The years had closed in and joined together. You could drown so many things in noise and laughter: awkward moments in the present that cried out for explanation, and yet could never be explained; sour memories out of the past; the strong-legged, red-headed girl dead in a Belfast sanatorium.

When Peter pulled back the curtains and stepped out on to the floor, Carson, again led the cheering.

"God, Peter," he said, "you fall somewhere between an undertaker and a professional footballer. Here, take a seat. Squeeze in here beside May. Your clothes won't take up much space. Mandy was going to give us a story when you burst in on us."

"Flowed in," said May. "What did happen to you Peter?"

"Walk by night and sleep by day," said Mandy's nephew, eyeing the roundness of May with undisguised appreciation. Carson laughed again, cocked a satirical thumb behind the nephew's back, led the whole company in a gale of laughter. May made room for Peter on a wooden bench at one corner of the fire. The heat licked pleasantly around his half-covered legs. At the other corner Mandy sat cross-legged on a low chair, slowly scraped out the bowl of his pipe with a broken-bladed knife.

"The story now," said Carson. "Mandy man, we want the story."

Mandy slowly refilled the pipe. "Seven hours, as I was saying, Jim boy. Seven hours I kept the boy from the folklore commission. Seven hours all in all cooling his backside on the rocks where I was herding the cattle. I told him a story Jimmy's Dan read for me out o' a tiny, wee paper-covered book. Sure the boy was as pleased as if Fionn himself or Conan the Bald had written the story."

"That won't do for us," said Carson. "We want the real stuff."

"You'll get it, Jim boy. You'll get it."

"Always remember there are ladies present. No stories about what you did when you were going to the dogs over in Roxburghshire."

"On my solemn oath, Seamus, I won't let out a word about Scotland. Not a blessed word. I'll give you a true story about a lad that was born west there near Burtonport."

"Go on then."

"Well, there was this man, a poor man, living west there near Burtonport. He had a wife and one infant, as fine a baby boy as you ever laid eyes on. The man died and the widow was left on her own to look after the infant . . ."

Peter, Carson, Davy, one or two others in the gathering knew the story, the simple, prosaic opening, the Homeric gesture that coloured the details, mingled the lives and sufferings of the people with the great, inconsequential progress of the picaresque. Mandy said simply: "It was the time of the evictions;" and only God knew what humiliating agony of a past generation was compressed artistically into that one sentence. Mandy could hold his audience. They leaned forward attentively. The red flames of the fire might have burned upwards from a hundred ruined homes, the soldiers closing in slowly around that one particular home to find only an infant in the cradle, helpless and innocent and utterly alone. Then a kind- hearted soldier brought the child away with him to the great city, reared and schooled it until it grew up to be a fine boy, and took to sailing the seas in a ship that was broken on the shores of Spain. He wandered the roads of Spain until, by an unfortunate accident, he was taken in the company of two robbers and locked up in prison. One day the two robbers made a plot to break free from the prison, abduct the daughter of the King of Spain, and make off with her to the desolate mountains. The lad overheard the plot, followed the robbers and their captive all the way to the mountains, rescued the maiden, killed the robbers, and brought back to the King's palace the fair daughter of the King. And the King in his regal joy called the priest, who married the girl to the lad that was born west there in Burtonport.

It was as simple as all that. Mandy clapped his knee with his flattened palm in a gesture as final as the fall of a curtain. He moved his chair back from the fire, made several sudden and irrelevant exclamations, caressed his baldness, spat forcefully into the ashes.

"Bully man, Mandy," said Davy.

"She must have been a nice piece," said Carson.

Peter could see her; not in one tale but in a hundred, in sad songs and gay songs, wise songs and foolish songs, her beauty put the last touch to the story or the last lilt to the tune. Gaelic folklore was filled with her presence. She sat in the glow of every hearth; the woman from Spain, from the land of the sun. Running through the legend of her beauty was the vision of the Spanish sword that might be the decisive, liberating thing. Spanish ale would bring hope. Bearded sailormen with vinous breath came back with stories of Spain to the narrow streets of little western towns—Ballyshannon, Kinsale, Killala, Westport, Galway. Now the little vessels were gone. The desire of beauty, the hope of the sword were buried behind the grey walls of old crumbling warehouses or on deserted grassgrown quaysides. Life moved in the air, on the water, under the water, with menacing metallic power. Death came drifting in casually, bobbing up and down with the advance and retreat of the waves, hideously bloated and swollen, torn against rocks, sprawled stiffly on the white sand. Mandy spat, slapped his knees, inserted his own naïve inventions into stories that burned with the passions of men dead for centuries. Fionn and Oisin and Conan the Bald, Diarmuid and red Grainne, Goll who wrestled with God on the Fenian meadows, jostled with clever third sons, slightly obscene giants, maidens from royal Spain, evicting soldiers, lads from Burtonport, potato-pickers in Ayrshire or Roxburghshire. Teachers from Belfast and civil servants from Dublin, holiday-makers and earnest students sat round in circles and listened. It was part of the national resurgence. Without a language, without nationhood Pearse had said "Ireland Gaelic and Ireland free." The King of Spain's daughter. The flag of Tone's republic above the burning post office in Dublin in 1916. Conolly the internationalist dying like a prince for the freedom of one small nation.

What under God did it all mean ? Had any people on earth put forward so many complicated claims to what the world called nationalism? Had any people on earth. . . . Look at the Yanks. I am proud and happy to be an American citizen, to fight a war to make helicopters available to every man, television to every family, kitchen gadgets to every American housewife. America would fight all right. Then, look at the British. Just look at them. Pride in their port, defiance in their eye. Or could any Irishman ever really see the British. They were so near to one. They irritated the eye. Some day he would write a book on the English problem.

"Listen," said Carson. "There they go."

The British were so near one. Going past now above the small fields, the stone walls, the rocks, the rough coast, the innumerable islands. One. Two. Three. The planes roared past somewhere in the darkness, over Mandy and the Burtonport lad and the King of Spain's daughter; over Carson who heard only the noise of a train and saw the girls running for it; over Davy who saw a girl in a white dress walking towards him, then lost the vision and brooded on the winged power of the oppressor, and saw the figure of his brother slightly ridiculous in football togs and a tailed coat.

Somebody said vaguely: "Atlantic patrol."

"You know W. B. Yeats's poem, Peter? The one about the Irish airman?" said May Harrison.

"I do."

"I always think of it when I hear an aeroplane. Yeats really was a great poet."

"He was."

"I love the lake isle. With low sound by the shore. Or the song of wandering Aengus. Golden apples of the sun."

"It's want of sleep, May," said Carson. "You'll feel much better in the morning."

"You shut up, Jim Carson. You've no soul. All you Strawberry Hill people are the same."

Carson unhooked Peter's trousers from the brace. They were wrinkled and warm and dry. He laid them on May's tight silky lap. He intoned: "Tread softly, May Harrison, you tread on Peter's best pants. A poet can offer no more. Why, May, we learned our poetry in Strawberry Hill. Even Mr. Eliot from New England. Stand on the topmost something of the stair. I shall wear the bottoms of my trousers rolled."

He dangled Peter's garment before the company.

"Jim Carson," said May, "you're as drunk as a lord."

Peter rescued his pants, gathered his clothes together, retreated modestly behind the curtain. Carson burst into song, leading the company in a chorus. The words were supposed to be spoken by a young woman who was married to an old man. She didn't like the general idea of being married to an old man. In particular she detested the old man she had married. The books of songs never gave the full forty verses, never printed the chorus as Carson sang it. After a few minutes it ended in laughter. The young wife and the withered husband vanished like a picture removed by a screen-dissolve. The singing began again. Behind the curtain Peter translated one verse:

> I cried last night at the little door in the distance,
> And I cried again on the love of my heart, my joy,
> Till her mother came and told me over the threshold
> She had slipped away in the night with the brown-haired
> boy.

The door was open and Carson was leading the company down the wet road. The storm had passed. There was a moon, a handful of stars, wisps of cloud scutched and scattered by the tempest. The roar of the swollen river died away behind them. The lake reflected the moon and the stars and the scattered clouds. The wet roofs and rocks glistened like great snailmarks. The dogs barked from house to house, out beyond the college, the sand-dunes; out to the headland and the last house on the edge of the sea.

VII

The day before the college closed was the day for the big excursion. All the boats in the place were hired, filled with students and teachers, pointed out with the first tide to the open sea and the islands. The white sails bobbed and dipped and disappeared out over the blue water. The sound of laughing and singing was blown back to the mainland, to the empty college with open doors and windows letting in the wind and sunlight; the stiff, empty benches, the dusty floor, the rickety piano, the chalkmarked blackboards, seemed to know the quiet day that heralded the long, cold silence of winter.

Hudie sat at the tiller watching the water with apprehensive eyes, telling Peter that sensible people would stay at home on the mainland. Ten miles down the coast a mine had washed maliciously out of the sea, burst on the rocks, smashed all the windows in the locality. God only knew what an unfortunate boat might strike against. The fishermen had sense, stayed at home, dined on tinned Canadian salmon purchased with money sent home from a son or daughter working in England. Peter heard Hudie's lament at spasmodic intervals in the singing and shouting of the passengers in the boat. Jim Carson, balanced perilously on the bow, led and guided the choral efforts. Davy sat close to the mast. Davy had not visited the college since the day they walked to the River Hotel. Even to-day he did not attempt to force his company on Rita. He avoided Peter.

She had come over for the excursion, walking quietly into Hudie's house before Carson or Peter or the Belfast school-teacher were out of bed. The clerical student from Armagh ate a meditative breakfast, spoke to her in conscientious Gaelic, helped her over the difficulties of conversation.

"Two weeks here and you'd be proficient," he said.

"Two weeks here and I'd be crazy."

The woman of the house and the servant-girl laughed in high good-humour. They liked the girl in the white dress. Her visits gave them a basis for quick banter, subtle jokes when the men were all together in the house. Peter accepted their fun. It was meant in compliment. It would pass around the college gossip-circuit, come eventually to Davy, save the trouble of awkward announcement or explanation.

The island came at them suddenly over ridge after ridge of tossing blue water. A few curious children watched the beaching of the boats, moved back timidly as the visitors crowded up the grassy slope, then closed in again when the fires were lighted and the eating began. A donkey with swinging creels padded up the track towards the cluster of white houses where the islandmen lived. A barefooted, white-headed boy ran behind it, shouting and waving a stick. An old, shawled woman stopped to look at the strangers, gave them a blessing and a wave of her hand, went on in the wake of the patient donkey and the shouting boy. The fires crackled, pale flames fighting the light of the sun. It was all curiously unreal, transient, but very pleasant and vibrant with peace, satisfying with the feeling of difficulties overcome, problems solved or at any rate temporarily abandoned to the vexed, complicated mainland. The soul was on an island, a green island in the deep wide sea of poor Percy Bysshe Shelley. The soul had found certainty and solid satisfaction.

Peter and Rita went alone up the track past the white houses. The doors of the houses were closed against the blistering heat of the sun. Down below on the sheltery side of the island the men and women worked at their small patches of ripe grass. Some of the visitors went down to them, went leaping over ditches, clambering over stone walls, to be greeted by cries of welcome from the workers, excited barking from the dogs. The path went up over rough heather and between rocks to the crumbling tower on the highest point of the island. They sat together at the foot of the tower, looking out across the water to the white line of surf that fringed the mainland, to the white specks that were homes where people lived, to the wall of conical mountains that shut off the rest of Ireland, the rest of the world.

"This is a day to remember, Peter."

"Every day from this out is a day to remember."

"This place is like Paradise. The sun. The blue sea. The quiet movements of the people."

"We're only visitors. Think of the storm. The boats lost. The keening in a dozen homes."

"Cheer me up, do! Tell me about our little home town. Soldiers and military lorries up and down the street from morning to night. As much curiosity . . ."

"I don't mean that. I mean Dublin. I'll have a job there in six or seven week's time."

"What do I do ? Keep on teaching dancing. Helping father in the shop."

"You can come with me."

"Peter, you're joking."

"I'm dead serious. What do we want to wait for? "We can get married, can't we?"

"But we're not on our own. There are people. Your people. My people."

"They'll manage."

"They'll object."

"If they don't know until it's all over they can't raise any objections."

"Here's one coming now that will raise objections."

The visitors who had not gone to help at the hay-making were dotting the little beach, plunging out against the sparkling advance of the waves. All except one who came up by the white houses, up the track towards the tower. They didn't speak as they watched his slow ascent, hidden now and again behind a heathery hillock or a straight wall of rock. The meeting was inevitable, anyway. They knew that. He knew it. He didn't pretend to be surprised at finding them there together.

"You didn't go swimming, Davy," she said.

"No, Rita. I don't feel in swimming form. I'm going back on the first boat so I came up to say good-bye. You'll all be leaving tomorrow."

"We'll see you there soon," Rita said. "When things blow over."

"Maybe. Whether they blow over or not." He turned away from them, walked a few steps, then came back suddenly.

"You're not saying anything, Peter."

"What do you want me to say? Talk about the weather?"

"No. I don't expect you to say anything about the weather. I thought you might stand up and tell us what a hound you are."

She stood up between them. She said: "Davy, have sense."

"I'm having sense. What right had he to come back and smash up everything that was between us? The spoiled priest. It was a lucky day for the Church when they advised him to leave the college."

"Davy," she said, "this isn't doing any good."

"I know it isn't doing any good. But, God, it's time somebody spoke the truth to . . . Melchisidech there . . . to yourself, Rita Keenan. You made a promise. Didn't you?"

"It would only be foolishness. Better to finish it now."

"Yes. It would be foolishness. I'm not God's gift to any woman at the moment. He has his prospects. His posh friends will plant him in a good job. He'll make money."

"It isn't just money, Davy."

Davy didn't answer. He turned his back on them and walked steadily back towards the beach. Peter said nothing. He looked down on the tiny bathers splashing in the surf, on the first boat going out from the little harbour, going back over the water to the mainland and the homes of men. They saw Davy at the dance in the college that night, the last dance of the season. Between dances he sat far away from them at the other side of the room. The music and dancing had about it the exuberance of the last, final celebration. The people of the place crowded about the door and there was handshaking, hearty farewells, hopes and wishes for the years to come. Half a dozen lads from a neighbouring village scuffled and catcalled at an open window until the priest in charge seized his stick and chased them ignominiously down the white road past the post office.

The moon came up out of the sea, shone on the distant islands, outlined the hill and the tower on the island where the men and women, weary with work and tanned with the sun, closed the doors of their white houses on the moonlight, on the sound of sea, on the whole world.

VIII

Peter and Rita watched the last bus leave from the corner where the road curved around the post office. Then they took their bicycles from the shady place between the gable wall of the building and the black stack of turf, and cycled down the road after the bus. A woman working in a garden or a man digging in a small potato-patch would straighten up as they passed and wave good-bye.

Rita said: "Should we go out of our way to see him?"

Peter doubtfully shook his head: "Wouldn't do any good. You can't argue with Davy. He gets an idea and there you are. He'll probably follow us home."

"Couldn't we persuade him not to? It'd be dangerous."

"He's my brother, Rita. Nobody could persuade him. Not while he's burning with the indignation of a just man wronged."

"I'm sorry about it all."

"Of course. But what could we do? There are some knots too entangled to be loosened. You must cut them."

"Well, we cut this one."

They laughed, free-wheeling together down a steep hill; down below them was the sea; up above and on their left the conical mountains stepped backwards and diminished. The wheels hummed musically. The wind sang in their ears. Down the coast to Bundoran was a long day's ride, past Dungloe where some time in the eighteen-eighties the authoress of *John Halifax, Gentleman* had marvelled at the hardihood of the man who built a town in such a wilderness. When Dinah Mary passed that way and wrote her book about wild Ireland there was a boy child in one of the roadside hovels, ready maybe for his first hired job with a farmer or his first journey to the Scotch potato-fields. The boy grew up in a changing world where new ideas had set the country seething like a boiling pot. He gathered the poor people about him for their own protection against poverty and rapacious grocers, had the hardihood to build in that wilderness a co-operative store. Later he wrote a book about his struggles with that waste of grey rock, with the more appalling waste and wilderness in the hearts of men. Over in England, more than fifty years after Dinah Mary Craik, they read and admired that book.

Then past Dungloe there was the long beauty of Gweebara bay, and the rocky townland named after the Wards, who were a race of poets. There was the sleepy town of Glenties in a hollow of the hills, and the road over the mountains to Inver by the sea, and to the strange little village of Frosses with the church and graveyard filling one side of the street. Once upon a time Inver men clearing a bog for the turf-cutting had come upon the dead body of a foreign lady, dressed in Spanish style, embalmed and preserved in the cool peaty soil. Nobody knew where she had come from. When the dress she wore had been in fashion the country around Inver was not even inhabited.

Rita wrinkled her nose at the story: "Very strange," she said.

"Like the *Marie Celeste*. But what does it matter now?"

"What does anything matter?"

He caught her hand as they rushed forward down another hill.

"Maybe it was the King of Spain's daughter," he said. "The one that married the lad that was born west there in Burtonport."

He aped Mandy's manner, his careful mouthing of awkward words.

"What about the Armada ?" she asked.

"The commonplace explanation. Anything queer that the centuries have left between Donegal and Kerry, anywhere along this western coast, the explanation always is the Armada. If you see a dark-haired woman at Galway races, somebody says the Armada."

"The Spanish sailors must have had a good deal of shore leave."

"Poor Spanish lady. Buried in the bog. I wonder how she got there."

"Don't worry, Peter. She doesn't mind any more."

She sang as they cycled: "*As I went down through Dublin city at the hour of twelve o' the night.*"

He bellowed in answer: "*Who should I see but a Spanish lady combing her hair by candlelight.*"

He said: "Do you know Higgins's poem about the Spanish man?"

"I'm tired of Spain. We'll sing something French, or American, or even Irish."

"No, listen, Rita."

He shouted the words into the wind that blew against their faces: "*My love I saw under still boughs . . . There were lovely ladies along the Claddagh . . . With quiet feet in your blue pampooties.*" The boats moved over the smooth water. The women sat in green gardens under cool branches. The lover told his love and was rejected. The fair one went off with the Spanish man.

Then they were cycling into Donegal town. The evening light was yellowing the houses around the diamond, the old walls of the castle by the bridge, the narrow lanes running down to the river. In such a light of exquisite evening Peter could imagine the four seventeenth-century friars bending over their manuscripts, chronicling carefully the past of a Gaelic world going down around them like a rotten wall. In such a light, maybe, the exiled Red Hugh O'Donnell died in Spanish Simancas, remembering the conical mountains and the waste of grey rocks, hearing the voice of that river going past a castle and an abbey to the wide sea.

Rested and refreshed they cycled down the road towards Ballyshannon. It was a lovely journey, a joyful journey, filled with memories and ideas, songs and verse and the sweet taste of beautiful things. They were going back to something that was worth going back to, not to a town that squinted by day and went by night into a gloom without stars. The sunlight would dance on the ridged roofs, the pigeons wheel in blue circles. They were going forward to something worth hoping for; lights and friends and the quick movement of life in a city.

Ballyshannon in the dusk balanced dizzily over the wide Erne. They went down the hilly street, over the great bridge, past the plaque to the poet Allingham, then along the road to Bundoran. Behind them the crash of the falling water at Assaroe went backwards into the night, was lost in the trampling advance of the great Atlantic. Peter's mother and father were in Bundoran on their annual holiday with Jack and Mary. Rita's father was taking the salt breezes at a large hotel beyond the town. They separated to meet again in the morning on the high, grassy place beyond the strand. They sat together in a glass-and-wood shelter that creaked before the burly force of the wind. Beyond the long, sprawling town were the steep table-topped mountains where Fionn had coldly watched the death of Diarmuid who had robbed him of red Grainne. Brothers in that brotherhood of legendary Fenian heroes, a red-headed woman had driven them asunder.

"Only a legend, Peter," she said.

"But very beautiful."

"I don't know. That Grainne was some hep-kitten. She certainly gave them all the run-around."

"You're going American."

"It's the cinema. You're going Gaelic."

"Reading Yeats maybe; That was his country over there. Beyond the water."

"Don't, Peter don't. I see the quotation dancing on your tongue."

He laughed. He looked down at the red half-moon of sand, the great waves advancing and rising and toppling, pierced by the sun, twisted by the rocks and the great wind.

"Could you guess what quotation it is?"

"Maybe," she said. "The one about the waves. *You waves though you dance by my feet like children at play.*"

He chanted: "*Though you glow and you glance, though you purr and you dart.*"

They laughed together. He kissed her and she clung to him with sudden vehemence. They were going over the waves and beyond the square mountains to something so desirable that longing sharpened into positive pain; to calm sunlight, blue circling pigeons, active crowds going up and down on wide, lighted pavements; to something that they wanted but that they were afraid to speak of aloud or to think of in their own minds.

6

The Gun

I

One picture showed the long line of men zigzagging down the beach between the burning town and the sea. The sea was refuge. The sea was escape from the flames behind them, from the grey hordes advancing, from the scream of engines in the air above, from bombs and machine-gun bullets. The long line waded out into the water to welcome the ships. Peter was reminded of a Harleian manuscript picture reproduced in some book of history, showing the ships that brought food to the army that Richard the Second had mismanaged in his Irish war. Green land, grey sea, embroidered sky. Three ships on the water and two men in each ship. Four coloured soldiers on the green land, two white tents, ten spears standing erect. Three coloured soldiers wading into the water, one of them accepting a round, brown bun from the outstretched hand of a man in the foremost ship. The delightful symbolism turned so much hunger and misery into something comically quaint. But the pitiless camera caught and made permanent all the dull horror of that slow zigzagging down the Dunkirk beach. Another picture showed an unshaven soldier crumpled in sleep in the corner of a railway carriage. A third picture showed a crowded corner of the deck of a transport ship, soldiers with faces bandaged, arms in slings, soldiers hopping on crutches, leaning on sticks.

It was a change from ancient tales about the Fenians, more modern tales about the King of Spain's daughter, from fiddling and dancing until the sea whitened around the islands and the sun came up behind the conical mountains. Peter folded the magazine, stuffed it into the pocket of his overcoat, hooked his coat in the corridor that went along outside the classrooms.

"Give it back to me next week, won't you?" said the history teacher. "Best collection of war pictures I've seen up to date."

"They're good all right."

"Terrible business, war," said the classics teacher.

The bell rang and they went into the classrooms. Peter opened the text-book and faced the class. Talking and whispering died down very gradually. When he, a few years ago, had sat in those desks as a senior boy, they had been junior boys in the primary school across the courtyard. Most of them remembered him distinctly, regarded him with a little awe, some with dangerous familiarity. They shuffled the pages of their books. Anyway, they knew he was only temporary, a month or so until Mr. Maconville's broken leg was knit together again.

"Page nineteen," he said. "Gregory. Stand out and read."

Gregory sat where Jim Carson used to sit. He stood out on the floor between his desk and the goldpainted radiator exactly where Carson used to stand when called upon to read or to wrestle with Livy or Horace. It was uncanny: the same room, the same landscape hanging on the wall, the same view out over the convent field.Gregory read resoundingly. He was a small, freckled boy.

"*Children love to listen to stories about their elders when they were children; to stretch their imagination to the conception of a traditionary great-uncle, or grand-dame, whom they never saw.*"

The last echoes of the bell thinned along the corridor, circled around the room, were absorbed in the resonance of Gregory's voice. Peter leaned on his desk, his head on his hands, heard the boy's voice like a bell booming down long, dark corridors, under the creaking branches of ancient cedars, around classical statues left curiously isolated and alone in a new world. A page of pictures showed streets on fire in Namur, dead horses huddled on the cobbles. Poor Elia and his dream-children; writing down his loneliness in immortal words to be read resonantly by freckled Gregory standing where Carson used to stand by the golden radiator. Dream-children? Carson would have his dream-children haunting his loneliness. Dream-children and children born of the dream of love roasted alive maybe in the wrecked streets of Namur. Davy would have his dream-children.

"*We are not of Alice, nor of thee, nor are we children at all. The children of Alice call Bartrum father. . . We are only what might have been, and must wait upon the tedious shores of Lethe millions of ages before we have existence, and a name.*"

Gregory was growing hoarse, reading with valiant resonance, glancing occasionally at the teacher and wondering when relief would come. He read the last sentence, coughed discreetly and provoked a few discreet sniggers. The teacher was asleep. They couldn't blame him. The day was warm, the sun bright on the convent field, the sky steadily and silently blue. A temporary teacher didn't need to kill himself. He wasn't there when the results came out. Gregory, increasingly daring, read the last paragraph all over again. Peter watched them with mild interest, shading his eyes with his clasped hands and wondering what Carson would have done under similar circumstances. The sniggers increased. Gregory sat down.

"Now, boys," said Peter, "pass me up your criticisms on the essay. One by one, please. Come up to me at the desk here."

He read the criticisms as they were carried up and laid before him; feet clumping up the floor; faces with the first faint beard beginning to show; the dusty smell of schoolboys. Then the bell rang again. They stood up and Peter recited the litany of the Blessed Virgin. They answered in mechanical sing-song, eyes wandering to the green grass and the slanting lines of evening sunlight. Then they stampeded to the door, scuffling, grabbing satchels, and swinging them recklessly, bursting out to join the liberated hordes from the other classrooms. In the corridor he draped his overcoat over his arm, went down the long quadrangle to the school gates.

"Next week, Peter. Don't forget," the history teacher called after him.

At the bottom of the playground he had a choice of two exits: one through a wicket gate opening on a narrow path that curved around a graveyard and went up under the shadow of the great walls and tall spires of the parish church to the town. Another wide iron gate, with a small door inset, let him out into a narrow back lane hot and smelly with the power of the sun. Ragged childern played around dishwatery doorsteps. Eyes looked out at him from small shady kitchens. The silence was heavy and sullen, absorbing the small voices of the children as trickles of water are absorbed by dry sand. This was as low as he could go in his native town; right down to the begging letters and petty theft, one or two suspicious characters, one or two loose reputations, and all around them, like the charity of Christ around the sins of Magdalen, the patience, the charity, the astounding spiritual life of the Irish poor. In every dark kitchen the red lamp of love burned before the picture of the Sacred Heart. A foreigner might see a red lamp, and jocosely guess mischief. But to the understanding eye it was a symbol of another life that ran like a hidden river under the struggles of degraded poverty; sweeping along with it the praying women in the Dublin slums, the story of the Dublin labourer who wrestled with evil and invisible powers on the very steps of the house of God; running on into a life that continued when poverty and degradation were forgotten, into eternity. Of course the thing had been sentimentalised in a hundred thousand pious pamphlets. He had himself lost a really firm grip on the reality that made possible the strong, everlasting life, on the thing symbolised by the red lamp and the holy picture in homes as poor as the carpenter's home in Nazareth. If he hadn't lost that grip he would be at this moment—he checked the idea against the dial of his watch—standing up after the noonday examination of conscience, walking down the smooth stone stairs, one black figure in a long black line, to dinner in the cool white refectory, listening to the reader in the rostrum shouting down the rattle of knives and forks with some beneficial spiritual reading, looking through the window at the flat green grass going off under tall trees towards the lake. Most of the time he knew he had lost that grip, and he accepted the position. And then suddenly in the warm stench of a poverty-stricken lane he staggered before that irrevocable decision, the agony of the dark nights of the winter, regretted the whole liberation of the sea and the sun.

A child stumbled and fell at the corner of the lane, cut the lazy silence with its thin cry. He picked up the dirty, squalling brat, steadied it on its feet, soothed it. Somebody came running over the threshold of the shop that filled the corner where the lane joined a steep street. A voice said: "Don't bother your head, sir. She's always falling."

He looked up and said: "How do you do, Josie?"

"Very well, Mr. Quinn."

Maybe, he thought, it's the job gives me status. That night in the ditch up near the quarry she called me by my name.

"Your child?"
"God forgive you, Mr. Quinn. I'm not married."
"What about Taffy?"
"Poor Taffy's as dead as a doornail. He was sent out to France.
"Maybe he's not dead."
"His name was on the list. It's the mistress's child."
"Who's the mistress?"
"Her man owns the shop. I work here."
A narrow passage ran down the middle of the shop. Rows of cramped snugs lined the walls. Behind the counter at the end furthest from the street were the ovens that fried the chipped potatoes and the slightly damaged fish. In spite of the stale smell it looked invitingly cool.
"Anything in there worth drinking, Josie?"
"Depends on what you like to drink. Nothing strong. Lemonade. We sell it with the chips."
"Sell me some now. And some sweets for the youngster."
"Nothing doing. No sweets. Anyway, that brat, Mr. Quinn. It's my torment."
They went up the narrow passage between the snugs, abandoning the child to the possibility of another tumble. Josie poured the lemonade into a cloudy tumbler.
"One for yourself, Josie."
She poured the second tumbler, blushing slightly. Customers were seldom so considerate. He admired her as she bent down behind the counter to drop the two empty bottles into a wooden crate. She was shapely. He could understand poor dead Taffy's passion; growing up to manhood somewhere between Wrexham and Swansea, finding his vision of beauty in an Irish town and behind the counter of a fish-and-chip saloon, dying miserably on the terrible French shore. Taffy was a Welshman and Taffy is a corpse. But Taffy had had eyes in is head.
She straightened up, leaned her bare elbows on the worn counter, sighed as she sipped her drink, with the sigh of one weary, relaxing into merited rest.
"Hard work, Josie?"
"Not so bad. I can take it. The boss is O.K. But the mistress is a divil. And that child. There's an off-day every week."
"You go out places?"

"When I've the money or somebody to take me. The rest of the time they go off an' leave me the shop an' the child to mind."

"Lonely for Taffy?"

"Sometimes. He was a harmless wee fellow. Still, I couldn't marry him."

"Why not?"

"He wasn't my type. Too much like everybody else. Too serious. People don't understand fun any more."

Her face wrinkled into a seriousness that was more than mature.

"You're not the first that said that, Josie."

"Maybe not. Maybe you read it in a book. But it's as true as God all the same."

"Am I your type?"

"You might be. But you'll marry Miss Keenan. She's mad about you, anyway. Always was."

"You know a lot, Josie."

"You can't help hearing it. Here in the shop. Or even when I go out walking. People come to me and tell me things. The boss comes and tells me about the wife. Then he tells me his ambitions and tries to put his arm about me. I don't mind him. He's harmless."

"What's his ambition?"

"Mostly gettin' his arm about me. Then he wants to change this place into one of those places you see in the pictures. People eatin' at tables, a dance band, a girl singin' in an' out between the tables, two dancers swinging each other round by the heels."

"Sounds good."

"Wouldn't work here, though. The people would laugh at you. The parish priest would soon put a finish to it. It'd be fun, though. That's why I don't mind the boss. He has the right ideas."

"Even if he has to try them out on you?"

"He doesn't do any harm. He doesn't get much fun, God help him. One child an' nag for the rest of his life. He tells me all about it. People tell me things, Mr. Quinn. You know the lake that you come to if you go out the road past the creamery and the quarry?"

He disguised his quickening attention under a smile and a half-bow.

"On that road I first had the pleasure of making your acquaintance."

She smiled. She said: "I like you when you say things like that."

A man came into the shop, bought cigarettes, went out again, stepping carefully around the playing child.

"Last day off," she said, "I borrowed a bike and went for a spin out to that lake. It was lovely. I met an old fellow when I was taking the air there. Oh, a real old dafty. Hair all over his face. Big boots and no laces in them. He told me all his woes. Something about a house and some people that wouldn't leave him alone. I couldn't make much out of it. But he mentioned names. He mentioned Dick Slevin."

Peter settled his coat more firmly in the crook of his arm.

"What about Dick Slevin?"

"The whole town knows about Dick Slevin. Then the old fellow mentioned another name."

"Whose name?"

"Maybe you'd be mad at me for not minding my own business."

"What's it got to do with me?"

"Your brother's name, he said. Your brother Davy that used to work in the camp."

"That's funny."

"It's not my business, Mr. Quinn. I know Dick Slevin. If your brother was anywhere near him . . ."

"He's not."

"You know best. Still, if the old fellow told me he might tell others. You never know."

"You never do. Thanks all the same, Josie. You're worth your weight in gold."

"If you're goin' to see Miss Keenan there's a short way down our back steps and across the Red Lion yard."

He laughed. "Josie, you think of everything."

"All for a friend," she said. "I like you, Mr. Quinn. There's nobody in here. It's safe."

She led him through a dark kitchen and a narrow scullery to the top of a high flight of wooden steps. He pressed her hand, kissed her lightly, went slowly down the long, resounding steps. He was Mr. Quinn. The job had given him status. A loose step rattled under his foot. If Lanty told her, he would tell others. But Davy was farming in west Donegal. Dick Slevin was damned well fit to look after his own affairs. Davy was in Donegal. The gravelly ground grated under his feet. He waved good-bye and she waved in return.

Davy in Donegal. Suffering God. The lunatic. He stopped dazedly and looked back to the top of the wooden steps. But she had gone, so he went on across the yard.

II

The Red Lion yard was one of the relics of the nineteenth-century Red Lion coaching-inn. A modern hotel had put it out of business. The Red Lion hostelry had become the Red Lion Printing and Publishing Works. The vast yard had split up like a decayed empire suddenly subjected to furious external attack. No man had ever drawn a boundary or built a fence but it was understood that one piece belonged to this man, another piece to that man.

Sheds had been built here and there to garage cars or store goods. On one side the dusty, gravelly expanse was bounded by the backs of the houses of Main Street. Crossing the yard Peter could see in the distance the back windows of Keenan's house reflecting the sun; and the green-and-white dance hall perched dizzily above a steep flight of stone steps. Behind him were the backs of the houses of the steep street where the seller of fish and fried potatoes indulged his cabaret ambitions, complained of his nagging wife, made tentative, harmless advances to the white- headed Josie. Along the third side of the roughly triangular yard ran the railway, double-tracking past the sooty engine-shed and the creaking turntable, cutting through a steep embankment, emerging to bridge the river a hundred yards below the red metal structure that carried the road. The bright colour of that metal bridge had burned itself into Peter's memory: red metal, red huntsmen, a spinning black gramophone-record, a green-and-white dance hall, a girl dressed in some striking arrangement of black and white.

He crunched his way across the yard and ascended the stone steps. In the cobbled area outside the dance hall Rita's father and two other men examined and discussed the merits of a small brindled greyhound.

"Did she race at the trials?" asked old Keenan.

"I sent her to Belfast," said one of the men. "She bate all before her."

"She's a good bitch, boss," said the other man. "You could do worse."

They straightened up when they heard Peter's foot on the cobbles.

"Hallo, Peter," old Keenan said. Beads of perspiraion marked his smooth, flabby forehead. "You're just the man I wanted to see."

"Why? I'm not an authority on greyhounds."

The three men laughed. "A good brindle bitch, isn't she?" Old Keenan indicated the greyhound.

"I wouldn't know. She looks all right."

"Meet Alec MacCabe, Peter. Alec, this is Peter Quinn. A clever young man. You know Paddy."

Paddy the shop-hand nodded to Peter, fondled the greyhound's head.

"I'll be going now," said MacCabe. "Come over to-night to clinch the deal."

He went off up the cobbled yard and out through the hallway into the street: a tall, swarthy, heavily built man in the late sixties.

"Alec's nervous," said old Keenan. "The stomach's at him again. He never had good health."

Paddy spat emphatically on the cobbles.

"Healthy enough, boss, when he helped to murder the three lads at Ennismore, back in 'twenty, during the big Belfast riot. A bloody old special. They dragged three lads outa bed an' shot them to pieces. Pulled them along the road until the skin an' flesh ripped off their backs. Innocent lads that hadn't hand, act or part in republicanism. Oh, Alec has a curse on him. Those murderers all died bad deaths. One o' them drowned himself an' another choked on his food."

Through two open doors and the arch of the hallway they watched the big man cross the street, his hand shading his eyes from the sun, keeping a nervous lookout for rushing military lorries.

"The light o' heaven will never blind him," said Paddy. "He's the last of a rotten breed. But the young ones are nearly as bad. The war gave them the excuse to grow up with guns in their hands, even if they did keep well away from the real fighting. We'll have black nights an' bloody blankets yet."

"That's no talk, Paddy," reproved old Keenan. "Talk like that has this unfortunate country the way it is. Alec was a brave man. Whatever his politics were."

"What about Ennismore, boss?"

"He wasn't next or near the place on the night of the murders. I ought to know. I was on the police at the time."

"Somebody was there."

"Somebody was. All over the country then murder was as common as ditchwater. Back as far as history goes there was bloody murder in this country."

"So the police say," said Paddy, leading away the brindled bitch.

"Come in with me to the house, Peter, before I slay that Paddy fellow." He took Peter's elbow and panted up the cobbled slope into the shadow of the hallway. His soft, round face was comical with anger. Ascending the stairs ahead of Peter he monologued breathlessly: "That Paddy fellow. Why in hell I keep him I don't know. He's worse . . . worse than De Valera ever was. All liberty an' Ireland united an' Gaelic. Whose bread did that class o' talk ever butter? . . . still, he knows drapery an' he knows greyhounds. We must make allowances."

He halted on the landing and looked down at Peter. "You'll find that out, Peter boy, as you go on in years. Make allowances for everybody in the hope that they'll make allowances for you."

Thoughtfully Peter followed him into the living-room. Such a father and then such a daughter. The mother must have been a wonderful woman. Or maybe God made allowances, balanced things out; Emerson had something on the law of divine compensation.

Rita wasn't in the room and Peter knew better than to ask about her with any immediate bluntness. The old man obviously wanted to palaver, moving nervously up and down the hearth-rug, watching his reflection moving in unison in the heavy overmantel. The stiff figures in the portraits still stared out of white backgrounds at heavily cushioned chairs, fashionable forty years ago, at the grapes and flowers carved to ornament the sideboard.

The old man said: "Any word of Davy?"

"The last we heard he was doing all right."

"God help him. I'm sorry for the lad. He should have kept clear of that Dick Slevin. The whole town knew Dick would come to no good. He was born to break the law."

"Some people are that way," said Peter.

"Some people are, but Davy's not one of them. What came over the lad at all? Free Ireland bedad. They are always that way, the young fellows, marchin' and drillin' about sweet damn all. I saw them when I had the uniform on. Now they've a bit of the country free and all the good men dead in the graves."

"Not all."

"The most o' them. Don't tell me, lad. What's the use, I ask you? Six wee counties rotten with Orangemen an' a government that would drive the King of England into the Republican Army."

"That's what the young lads want to change, I suppose. Maybe their way isn't the right way."

"Begod it isn't. Sitting on your backside in gaol or loose like Dick Slevin with a price on your head."

"Good men have had a price on their heads."

"I know, lad. Priests and patriots. But I'm too old to argue with you. You're not a rebel yourself."

Peter struggled to disentangle one from the other the dozen possible answers. Not a rebel. Well, not against the great, vague undefined Red Thing. What was it? Where was it? Perhaps against the Orange Thing, its one narrow eye of self-interest looking narrowly on the world, its heavy inelastic mind, the fear of domination that drove it to dominate, the hobgoblins it imagined: rebels and Jesuits and intrigue from Rome. A rebel, perhaps, against the restraint that was sun, wind and warm rain to the white flowers in the walled garden. Perhaps against a town where curious eyes slanted out of ancient doorways, a life that persisted without change. Had this vague discontent no name: shadowy rebellion suggested by the shadow that was the negation of God?

The old man said: "Rita spoke to me about Davy."

Peter was attentive, ashamed of the way his mind twisted, searching to answer a question that needed no answer.

"She told me some time ago that there was something between them. I made out that he asked her to marry him an' she didn't turn him away."

"Why should she?"

"No reason at all, lad. No reason at all. Davy's a good lad. A hard-working tradesman can always make enough to live on. He can rise in the world if he watches his step. I was agreeable to let the girl have her own way. She's sensible."

"She is."

"I'd a feeling though she wasn't as content as a girl should be when she gets the man of her heart. And then Davy went and got himself into trouble."

"It makes a difference."

"It does. You can marry your daughter to a tradesman but not to a lad running with the police at his tail. The girl will worry herself to a breakdown."

"About Davy?"

"That's part of my trouble. I'm not right sure that her main worry is about Davy. I don't know. Rita's a strange girl. Quiet, the way her mother was."

"What other worry could she have?"

"I don't know, Peter. There's no way a father can understand the heart of a child. That's why I'm talking to you. The two o' you were great when you were children together. Maybe a friend could find out what a father couldn't. You watch them as children. Every thought of theirs is as plain as a spud on a plate. Then they're men or women hidden from you to the end of time. It's an awful thing to be the father of a family."

Many a man, thought Peter, had a larger family and less to feed them on, and still had wisdom enough to leave to his children the privacy of their own minds. How much exactly did the old man know ? What would be his reaction if he were suddenly and bluntly to be told the whole truth? You never knew quite how much canny duplicity might be hidden behind that round, perspiring face. A man didn't survive the troubled years as a policeman and then make a success of the drapery business, with a profitable sideline in racing dogs, without having in his disposition some cautious guile. He might give his consent to a marriage between his daughter and Peter Quinn, but it would be wary, provisional consent depending very much on how and when Peter Quinn began—God help us—to rise in the world. Looking at his potential father-in-law Peter felt sick and weak with anger and impatience. The man had tried to trap him into telling the truth, declaring his—again, God help us—intentions. Then with Peter at his mercy he could hum and haw his way from postponement to postponement. Well, he had still to learn a twist that neither a part in the policing of tumultuous Ireland nor a retirement spent in buying and selling dry goods had taught him. There was only one way to solve this problem; and the quicker Rita came to agree with him the better. He was impatient to have it all over and done with; the last letter from Dowdall that might arrive any of these days, the train journey to Dublin, that would leave Davy wherever in hell Davy wanted to be, imagining grievances, nursing his resentment; that would leave old Keenan to his brindled bitches and his bales of cloth and his wailing about the responsibilities of a father. God in heaven, but he was sick of it all: the town, the people, the streets, the river, the circle of hills, the blue pigeons, the towering steeples. He wanted to be miles away. At the moment he wanted, madly wanted, the door behind him to open and the girl to come into the room. Somehow she would make the place, even that place, live; would give it meaning, colour, beauty.

He said: "I see your point, Mr. Keenan; I'll do anything I can."

"Do you ever go to see the racing dogs, Peter?" asked old Keenan. "We've a good track here. As good as anything in Dublin or Belfast."

The sudden irrelevancy, a quick, crafty glance of assumed understanding, told Peter that the door really had opened behind him, that she was in the room. Then he saw her reflection in the overmantel, slightly distorted but still slim and strong and neat, alive with a sinewy, subtle attractiveness. He stood up and welcomed her with a smile.

"Don't start Peter on the dogs, Father," she said. "Next thing you know he'll be smoking a pipe."

"It's better sport any day than that tennis," said her father.

"Not so much exertion anyway, except for the dogs."

The old man laughed, eyed her with a fatherly, appreciative pride. Peter knew that he had another rival, more dangerous even than poor Davy hiding in Donegal . . . or wherever in hell Davy chose to hide.

III

Going down the dry sandy path to the tennis club Peter said: "There's only one way out of this place, Rita. The quicker we take it the better."

She said nothing. She walked on, with her eyes thoughtfully watching the spurts of soft sand dancing upwards from the light touch of her white tennis shoes.

"The longer we wait, Rita, the worse it gets. We're only

tormenting ourselves. Your father won't give his consent in a hundred years."

"What about your people?"

"They'll get used to the idea."

The tennis courts were in one corner of a level holm by the edge of the river. The path went around the edge of a football field to the green army-hut that served as a pavilion and clubhouse for the tennis players. Around one goal-mouth a dozen jerseyed lads carelessly punted a football, shouted and laughed in a manly defiance of all the milksoppery of lawn tennis. Sitting in the shade on the steps that went up to the door of the pavilion Peter watched Rita play a quick, graceful game against the ponderous lobbing and scooping of a grey-headed middle-aged matron. He followed the upward sweep of her right arm, the flash of the racket, the bounce of the ball from the taut strings. One of the raucous footballers deserted his companions, strolled across the grass to stand attentively looking at Rita's half of the game. Peter couldn't blame him. The last few months had emphasised the beauty that had always been somewhere in the girl, restrained and controlled but undeniably present. It needed only the sun and swift movement and a short tennis skirt to make her attractiveness obvious enough to draw a lad, growing his first beard, away from his own characteristic, callow delights.

The courts were practically deserted. Away beside the river four schoolgirls giggled over a slow game of doubles. Beyond the last court, on which they played, the cool, rapid water danced past, liberated from the town and the last bridge, curving northwards to loop the great holm where the soldiers had their playing- fields and firing ranges. Far away across the flat land a few brown figures moved, indistinct in the haze that the afternoon sun sucked up from the drying grass; and now and again a rifle cracked, the sound cutting through the stillness, disturbing the little, casual sounds of voices and laughter, the noise of the river.

"A great building, the barracks," said a voice behind Peter.

"It is, brother."

Brother Jones came out of the pavilion, clumped down the steps, seated himself comfortably on the cool grass. He was a small bald-headed man, crisp as the skin of a lemon. He looked across the river at the great grey barracks towering on a hill over the flat land. Behind the grey building they could see the spires and the highest roofs of the town.

"Stone was cheap when they built that place," said Brother Jones.

"It was," said Peter drowsily.

"It's like a castle, a castle of the Middle Ages."

Somewhere within the grey walls a bugle blared, shrill and distinct. The distant brown figures clustered together, moved at a steady march towards the barracks.

"A castle of the Middle Ages and a trumpet blown from its battlements. It must have been great to be alive then, Peter Quinn. There was more colour in life. Men were more sane."

"As sane as they are to-day or at any other time, brother. If it's colour you want could you beat what we have before us? The town, the soldiers, the river, the green grass, the tennis players, the footballers and their jerseys."

"You didn't mention my own black coat and my white collar. You're a bit of a cynic, Peter."

"So, they tell me. What it means exactly I don't know."

"I do. I taught you when you went to school, Peter. I don't know what the word means in the dictionary. I don't know for certain what the Wilde boyo meant when he said a cynic was a man who knew the price of everything and the value of nothing."

The old eyes wrinkled up at Peter, pale with an opaque shrewdness that was more than wisdom.

"But when I call you a cynic, I know what I mean. Even if I do use the wrong word."

"Let me have it, brother."

"The things that God sends to you, Peter, you keep putting away from you, postponing the taking of them because you're afraid that acceptance will be the beginning of a real bad disillusion."

"That might mean anything about anybody, brother."

"It might, but about you it's God's truth."

"Is it the whole truth? Suppose I saw something that I wanted more than anything else in the world. Suppose I defied the whole world, put out my hand and took what I wanted?"

"It wouldn't prove me either a liar or a fool. If God didn't want you to take that thing it might only mean genuine disillusion."

Peter wanted to ask jeeringly how he was to know when God did or did not want his servant, Peter Quinn, to take possession of this, that or the other thing. But then Brother Jones had taught him at school. Brother Jones was, while he continued to work as a temporary teacher, his legal superior. Above all the answers were so obvious, so painfully obvious, written down in black and white in the penny catechism. And inspiring that simple series of questions and answers, inspiring every code that stood between man and barbarism, was the law that said a man should take nothing that was not his own, should say or do nothing to leave misery and bitterness in the heart of another man. It was all too damned much for the head on a hot day. In a sudden feeling of irritation he could have kicked Brother Jones, rolled him over on the green grass, clerical clothes and clerical collar, lemon-crisp skin and shrewd eyes. He turned his eyes back to the girl in the short white skirt, to her active movements, her easy graceful stroke, to the shapely legs and nimble feet that brought to that game on green grass all the cool accuracy of a classical dance. Every movement of her body wrote words on the blue-green air. He could understand those words. They were simple and direct. They isolated Rita and himself from the rest of the world, from the laws of men and the laws of God, sweetly persuaded him to put aside the idea that was part of his bone, portion of his people and of all Christian people: no man, no woman is exempt from obedience to the law; no action can be isolated with the person or group that performs that action.

"Miss Keenan plays a very good game," said Brother Jones.

She moved swiftly, gracefully, each gesture of arm or leg telling him that they were alone, isolated by the tremendous importance of their love for each other. Brother Jones, his people, her father, melted into insignificance. They were alone and she moved only for him. His eyes were dazzled by that white appealing movement. He hid his face suddenly in his hands.

"The sun's strong," said Brother Jones, slithering closer to the wall of the pavilion.

"It is."

"Still, it's better than wet weather for the farmer at this time of the year. This day twelve months ago the river was high in a brown fresh. There isn't a drop too much in it to-day."

"There isn't."

"That's the way. One year a flood. Next year a drought. Year after year. How would you like to live teaching here year after year, Peter?"

"Wouldn't like it much."

"Well, mind you, you could do worse. And there'd always be an opening for you here if you went up to National and took your degree."

"Too much trouble."

"Not to a man with your intellect, Peter. You'd astound them up there."

"I don't want to astound anybody. I want a job, money coming in with some regularity."

"Well, there's a lot to be said for that. Maybe too many examinations and certificates and degrees have turned our heads in this country. There's a lot to be said for a job an' regular money. Have you any prospects?"

"I'll manage something soon in Dublin. I know a fellow there."

"There's nothing like knowing a fellow. It's the way to get on in this country."

"In every country."

The white arm rose, the racket flashed, the ball bounced backwards and forwards. Brother Jones stood up, meticulously dusted and smoothed the seat of his pants, restored his hat to his small, shining head.

"Still, Peter, I'd like to have you working under me permanently. You do your job well. It's an easy, quiet life too, in a town where everyone knows you and you know everyone. People respect you. They call you Professor when you're really only a teacher in a secondary school. You could live happily and die in peace."

"Dublin's a nice place."

"I know that. I was born there. I love every stone of Dublin, from the newest stone in the newest house in the newest garden estate to the oldest stone in Audoen's Arch. Still, it's a city, Peter. A small city. A Catholic city. But a city all the same. People always in a hurry. Big hotels here and stinking slums around the corner. Opportunities maybe for every man, but terrible temptations for every man as well."

"No different from any other place."

"Maybe not. Anyway, I'm old to be talking an' advising. But that's my job. Maybe it's the privilege of age. You could do good here."

"What good?"

"Well, there's social work to be done. The Saint Vincent de Paul Society. You know there are people needing help here in this town. Then there's the Legion of Mary. The dramatic society. The Gaelic League classes."

"They'll get along without me."

"They will. But intelligent young men are always welcome. 'Tisn't easy to keep things going in a place like this. These small-town jealousies are the devil."

The middle-aged matron played with a grim solidity, opposing herself doggedly to that quick movement and white flying grace. The footballers grew weary, pulled crumpled jackets over coloured jerseys, gathered to watch the tennis. Brother Jones doddered across the grass, nodded to the footballers who saluted him respectfully, went slowly away along the sanded path. Small-town jealousies and small-town social activities. Year after year. One season of flood and one season of drought. On and on until you doddered slowly across summer grass, and footballing boys, ugly with the first suspicion of a beard, saluted you respectfully. It was one way of growing old, passing from the red flare of dreams into the common light of common hours, back into the red flare again, bending low over the red fire, with only memories, vague memories. In such a mood phrases from Yeats came naturally to the mind, filling it with a proud melancholy that had nothing in common with a summer afternoon and a game of tennis drawing to an inevitable finish. The dogged matron threw up her hands and took her defeat laughingly. Rita danced lightly around the net and together they approached the pavilion.

"Will you play the winner, Peter?" asked the matron, removing an eyeshade, mopping perspiration from a muscular face.

"Nothing doing. She's too good for me. Anyway, it's too hot."

"Coward," chaffed Rita.

"He's wise," said the matron. "Never give a woman an advantage over you. You'll get along that way."

In the ladies' dressing-room they slipped off the short white skirts; mopped away the perspiration.

"He's a good boy, that," said the matron, watching Rita's strong, neat shoulders with envious admiration.

"He's all right."

"You mean more than that, don't you, Rita? He'll get on, that fellow. He's good-looking too."

She struggled with effort into a flimsy frock that clung with strain and desperation to the bold line of her figure. She combed her hair before the one tiny mirror.

"Thank God for your figure, Rita child," said she.

"I won't have it always."

"You will. You're not the fattening sort. Your mother, God rest her, was as light on her foot as a lamplighter."

They rejoined Peter outside the pavilion, Rita's hair fell loosely down on shoulders shapely in a coloured cotton blouse. They walked together back towards the town, leaving the footballers lying in an idle circle on the grass, blowing blue smoke into the quiet air. Beyond the river and behind the grey walls the bugle sounded again.

"Teatime for the rookies," said Rita.

"Not much sign of war here," said the matron. "This place is as peaceful as heaven."

"Will heaven really be peaceful?" asked Peter. "All those harps and things."

The soldiers swung around a street corner, marching irregularly, whistling a cinema hit to the syncopation of rattling mugs and plates. Around their feet a faint dust rose from the street.

"God help them," said Peter.

"They'll win yet," said the matron.

"They're somebody's sons," said Rita.

"Somebody's lovers," corrected the matron.

"Sons and lovers," said Peter. He added in explanation: "It's the name of a book."

IV

Jack and Mary came over for their tea, very noisy and very cheerful, filled with the joy of the good weather. Jack and old Quinn hobnobbed together in one corner of the kitchen, gossiping about the office, the funny things that happened there to vary the day's routine. A post office was not quite the same thing as any office. Twenty or thirty postmen went out every morning, returned in the evening with the gossip of all the country districts around the town.

Old Quinn coming near his retirement looked back over long years of that gathering and garnering gossip. Anecdotes came naturally from him; pouring out from a well-stocked, colourful memory. Jack exultant in a recent promotion listened with enthusiasm.

In the cool pantry Mary and her mother dressed salad for the tea. Mary, red head bobbing actively, whispered excitedly to her mother, who nodded at intervals with all the wise patience of experience. They didn't tell Peter what all the whispering and nodding was about. It was etiquette for women to discuss those matters only with familiars of their own sex and their husbands, leaving the rest of the world to guess as well as it could, knowing quite well that the rest of the world would guess with considerable accuracy. It was only in America—if one could accept the testimony of the movies—that young women startlingly announced approaching maternity to the assembled family circle or to anyone else that might happen to be present. Maybe that was just necessary on the screen for dramatic effect. Maybe the Americans were no different from anybody else; except in having a positive mania for homes and babies, in delightful contradiction to divorce laws that made a home as temporary as a tent.

Over the cool salad and the hot, sweet tea, Jack said: "How does the teaching agree with you, Peter?"

"It's not so bad."

"You should stick to it, now. It's a top-notch job. Short hours and long holidays."

Jack had become very much one of the family, feeling called upon to give advice, to offer his opinion. He meant no harm. Peter knew that. Still, it could be offensive. Mary looked understandingly at Peter, between her raised knife and fork. She had more in common with her brother than she would ever have in common with her husband. Love and the union of the flesh could never quite go down as deep as those strange atavistic understandings, communities of instinct and feeling. He would miss Mary when he had gone, and he felt with some gratified pride that her life would be poorer because of his going. She understood so much, took so much for granted, asked no unnecessary questions. But his silence told her more than his words told other people. His father was happy with Jack Carney's conversation. His mother had found new hope in the news that Mary had whispered to her in the pantry. Peter couldn't blame them if they seemed to have shut him out of their lives. He was no longer any part of their joy in the present or their hope for the future. To his mother he could only bring back and renew the awful sense of failure and disappointment. They would hardly miss him when he had gone. They had Jack and Mary. They would have their children. They would have Davy.

Davy's name came back to him as he walked after tea through the Diamond. There might possibly be nothing in it. In any case Peter didn't see what he could do about it. If Davy chose to come back to danger, then Davy was his own master.

He crossed Main Street in front of the picture-house, went between two parked military lorries to regain the footpath. The man leaning against the wall turned so quickly up an entry that Peter was not for a moment positive about his identity. But the sudden speed of his disappearance startled him into something like suspicion. He went up the entry, walking at a normal pace. You couldn't suddenly break into a sprint without making people curious. The entry tunnelled under a large three-story building, then swerved to the right underneath the picture-house, to run for fifty yards to a practically disused stable. Farmers nowadays came into town by bus, didn't need much accommodation for horses.

When he was out of sight of the street he began to run, gaining rapidly on the steps that shuffled on before him, very awkward and very audible. Every doubt had vanished even before he turned into an empty horsebox to see Jacob crouching backwards against the bare manger. The thin brown face scowled angrily at Peter. The body was more erect than it had been since Pete had died. A great effort had given some neatness to the clothes. The boots were laced and roughly polished.

Peter stood blocking the mouth of the horsebox.

"What's come over you, Jacob? Running away from an old friend as if you were running away from the police."

"I've no call to be afraid o' the police."

"I know that, Jacob. I was only joking."

"Why can't a body be left alone? I'm bothered at home. And when I come into the town I'm chased like a rabbit."

"Nobody chased you, Jacob. You wouldn't run away from an old friend."

"Why can't the people mind their own business?"

"Who bother you, Jacob? Surely you wouldn't say that I bother you."

The thin brown face relaxed gradually. The little eyes cooled to mildness. He came forward slowly from the manger.

"You're all right. But there's other ones that aren't next or near all right. When they're around you couldn't call your home your own."

"Who are they, Jacob?"

"Never mind that. I'll mention no names. But I know how to move them."

"You wouldn't turn them out, would you? Pete wouldn't have done anything like that."

"Pete was a big bully. But he's dead in the grave. I'll move them. I want the place for my own uses."

He moved forward, but Peter quietly blocked his way.

"You're tired, Jacob. Come home with me and have a good rest."

"I won't go home until I move them. Let me out past you, Peter Quinn."

"Now, Jacob, is that the way to talk to an old friend?"

He saw the blow coming and ducked backwards to avoid it. The stone grazed his jaw, crashing with surprising force against the opposite wall. Then Jacob was past him and running towards the street with an agility as suprising as the craft that had concealed the stone and the strength that had flung it. Peter ran a few steps in pursuit, then saw the futility of going back towards the street, the people, the police. At the other end of the stables a gate opened into a grass-grown lane that ran parallel to the main street. He climbed the gate, ran quickly along the deserted laneway, came back into the street a hundred yards away from the cinema. There was no sign of Jacob. Peter walked down the street, across a bridge, along a wide road lined with high-windowed expensive houses. Rita was waiting for him, leaning on the wooden bridge over which a narrow side-road led into the town's only public park. She looked up and smiled.

"Who's late this time?" she gibed.

He leaned breathlessly against the wooden railing of the bridge. He said: "I met poor Jacob. He did his best to brain me with a lump of stone. As sure as God he's in the town to tell the police."

"It's not your business, Peter. Dick Slevin can look after himself."

"I wasn't thinking of Dick Slevin, but Davy. I think Davy has come back."

"He wouldn't be so foolish."

"He's fool enough for anything."

His seriousness convinced her. She turned to him with a pale, terrified face.

"If it's true, Peter, it's my fault. We'll have to do something."

"Don't talk rot. He has nobody to blame but himself. We didn't invite him back."

"We'll have to warn him."

"I'll do it. You go home and wait for me. I'll tell you to-morrow how I got on."

He ran from her along the byroad that circled the park then wandered away under the cool silence of the trees. She followed him silently.

"God, Rita, this is no job for you. Go home."

"I won't. Anything might happen to you. There's safety in numbers."

"Rita, for God's sake."

"Don't waste time arguing. The police will be there before us."

"Oh, all right. You'll look sweet in Armagh gaol."

He walked on, giving her grudgingly the support of his arm.

"Now we look like a courting couple," she said. "Nobody would ever think we were stuffed full of treason and sedition."

He laughed, reluctantly admiring her spirit, her unassumed courage.

"Maybe," said he, "Jacob didn't get as far as the barracks yet. He's easily distracted. Maybe the police won't bother until it gets quite dark. None of them will be anxious to show themselves to Slevin in broad daylight. Wouldn't blame them."

The shadows gathered around them as they walked. The shadows thickened upwards under the trees, flowed smoothly out over the warm fields. They twisted and turned, up one byroad and down another. They short-cutted through gates and across fields, running and stumbling in the shadows when they thought they were unobserved, walking sedately when another person or two or three came towards them along the road. Then they turned the last corner and saw the wide lake very quiet between the smooth, round hills. The last light dripped delicately out of the sky, gathered delicately over the mirror of the water. They were both afraid, moving cautiously up the lane to the old house, listening attentively for the sound of voices, heavy footsteps, the hum of a motor, the sharp crack of a gun. Her hand found Peter's hand and gripped it tightly. But there was no sound except the water licking around grey rocks, little stones, green reeds; or the sleepy cry of a bird or the plop of a feeding fish. Then the house was before them, a shapeless shadow, a huddled ruin dominated by the great black barn. They stood still. There was no light, no sign of life.

She whispered: "Is it safe?" They waited for a few minutes, looking at the house until the objects detached themselves from surrounding shadows and stood out distinct and visible, listening until the noise of the lakewater came to them like a voice repeating again and again the same low cry. Then they advanced slowly towards the house. Peter rattled gently the crazy door. There was no answer. She called softly: "Davy. Dick Slevin." The house was dead silent. The water whispered around the reeds, rippled and broke on the stony shore.

"Hammer the door, Peter."

"No point in that. They'd hear us in the police barracks. The night's so quiet."

"They might be asleep."

"No. They're not there. They've noticed that Jacob has cleared out, maybe."

He walked to the window, bent down, vainly tried to see through the dust-covered panes. She leaned over his shoulder. "No future in that, Peter. You'd want an x-ray."

Then Dick Slevin's voice spoke just behind them. He had come silently around the corner of the house from the direction of the barn. He stood leaning casually against the dirty wall.

"Visitors," he said. "What the hell do you want?" They turned away from the window and he recognised them.

"I'm honoured," he said. "A pair of lovebirds. Suppose the police followed you the whole way."

Peter went towards him. "Slevin, there's no time for lip. Where's Davy?"

"How do you expect me to know?"

"He's here."

"Do you see him?"

"We know he's here."

"Who told you?"

"Jacob. He was heading for the barracks when I left him."

Slevin stiffened. "Christ, I knew he would. Davy's a fool. Davy sent him into the town with a letter for you." He pointed to Rita. "When I had the fool to myself I never let him outa my sight."

"Davy's here, then?"

"Here. I wish to hell he was at the bottom of the lake."

He led them across to the barn, running with short jerky strides; called through the open door into the damp, stale darkness: "Davy. Come out to hell. Jacob's gone for the cops." They heard the sound of Davy's feet falling and fumbling in the dark for the rungs of the ladder that came down from the barn-loft. Then he came out over the threshold, hesitant, untidy, brushing hay from his rumpled coat.

"Hello, Rita," he said. "I sent you a message."

"I didn't get it, Davy. Not yet."

"What in God's name brought you back here?" asked Peter. "Weren't you all right, where you were?"

"That's my own business."

"I hope you're as independent when the police get here."

"We'll manage the police without your brotherly help."

"That's not very nice, Davy," said Rita. "We came out here to help you."

"First-class," said Davy. He buttoned his jacket with deliberate care. "I wanted to talk to you anyway, Rita."

Slevin moved a few steps away from them, listened intently. "Do your talking some other time, Davy. This is where I begin to travel. Thanks, Peter, for the tip."

Across the water they heard the hum of a heavy engine, moving slowly towards the lane that led to the house. Slevin pointed towards a clump of trees huddled on the edge of the lake, drooping wearily over the quiet water. "Peter Quinn. There's a boat there. It's only an old flat-bottemed thing. But it'll carry yourself and the girl. Keep close to the far shore. You're safe enough in the dark. Davy, you come with me."

"I can look after myself."

"Come on, you fool. There's only one way you can go."

He gripped Davy by the arm, pulled him along with him. The noise of the engine had ceased. The silence was wicked with menace. Peter could see in his imagination the uniformed men coming silently, cautiously, deliberately along the rutted laneway. Rita muffled a scream that cracked out from strained nerves.

"Hysterics on all sides," said Slevin's voice. Somewhere in the darkness they heard the little snap of a safety-catch and then the night split wide open at the report of a revolver.

"That'll hold them," said Slevin. "They'll sit and think for a while now. Beat it, Peter. Come on, Davy."

Peter ran as quietly as he could towards the clump of drooping trees. He held Rita's arm, guiding her over the rough places, cursing Slevin's wild bravado from the bottom of his heart. Now the police would come running. He poled the awkward boat out a few yards from the shore, keeping in the shadows as well as he could, waiting in panic until the flat bottom would grate fixedly on stones or sand. There were no oars and the cumbersome pole splashed in the water with a sound that must be audible all around the lake. A hundred yards from the house he stopped, resting quietly on the pole. Rita sat very still in the bottom of the boat. There was no sound beyond the lapping, rocking movement of the water.

She whispered: "Peter, do you really think they'll get away?"

"At the moment I don't give a damn whether they do or not."

"They can't do anything to us. Even if they do catch us."

"Except shoot us by mistake. I don't feel like being shot by mistake."

"Peter, are you a coward?"

"I often wonder. Nowadays a man doesn't get a chance to find out. We're too civilised. We're too neutral."

"We're not neutral here in the Six Counties."

"In spirit we are. Except a few Orangemen. And in practice they're as neutral as Switzerland. They don't want any serious fighting. Anyway, war doesn't prove a man's courage. It's a mass hysteria. The bravest man I ever heard of was shot as a coward during the last war. Didn't like killing people. He died for his convictions."

He leaned on the pole. They moved on over the dark water until the boat grated on the pebbles of the far shore, fifty yards from the road. There was no sound of guns or motors or men; nothing but the tireless voice of the lake. Peter led the way, wading through the shallow water, going bent double in the shelter of ditches for a few hundred yards, following a course leading away from the lake and parallel to the road. Then turning to the right they followed a cart-track that went past the door of a silent, sleeping cottage. No light showed in the dull windows. No dog barked. A few hens squawked irritably in a wooden lean-to at the gable of the house. Then they were out safely on the road, walking towards the town, tramping and swinging their arms until heat and courage returned to their cramped, chilled bodies. Half a mile outside the town the police-lorry overtook them. Crouched in a gateway until it passed, they posed in the one attitude that was beyond suspicion of sedition. Her heart thumped against him. She said: "They've caught nobody, anyway." Her arms tightened about his neck. Her body shook with dry, stifled sobs. The perfume about her neck was strong and rich in his nostrils.

"You're tired out," he said.

She sobbed: "Thank God. Thank God. They've caught nobody. Peter, where will it all end? That poor boy. And we've hurt him, Peter."

"Come home, Rita. We'll go away out of this place and begin our own life."

"There's a curse on us."

"Not on us, child. On this place. On every place where men can't live together in peace. The curse that came on the sons of Adam when one of them killed his brother. Maybe that was what the poet meant when he talked about a land without stars.

She smiled at him suddenly. "Peter the poet. You'll quote to God when He judges you. What poet was that?"

"It doesn't matter. Maybe he was only a crabbed old man."

He held her very close to him, crushing her body with protective strength, looking down into the frightened, laughing face.

"Rita, you'll come with me. You must come. We'll get married in Dublin. We'll be on our own then. Our own life."

She said: "I will." She said: "If you were in hell I'd follow you there." She said: "I love you, Peter, I love you."

Then he kissed her until everything that had happened that night, and every other night and every other day, was only a dull, tedious memory.

V

Next weekend the Féis happened. It happened once a year, filling, three days out of three hundred and sixty-five with music and dancing and singing. Only at festival time did the divided life of the town become genuinely and painfully noticeable. On the twelfth day of July the Orangemen had, before the war folded the banners and silenced the drums, drummed and marched in procession, isolating themselves in remembrance of a glorious and immortal memory about which nobody else gave a twopenny damn. The annual Féis was a cultural festival, song and dance and music on the lines of a Welsh Eisteddfod, exhibitions of handicraft and rural arts. But because the name given to it was a Gaelic name, and because Gaelicism was associated with Nationalism, and because a nationalist was a man who believed Ireland was a nation, that very simple, harmless celebration split the town as effectively as if an earthquake had passed that way. As a general rule Catholics took part in it and Protestants didn't, for the line that divided religions also divided political allegiances.

Peter helped with the activities of the weekend, wondering vaguely, as he shepherded people to their seats in the town hall to watch the dancing contests, how an outsider—English, American, French or German—could possibly hope to understand clearly the politics of the small north-eastern corner of the small island on which the Irish people lived. The events of three centuries had added complication to complication: broken Gaelic chieftains, imported Presbyterian planters, an Orange organisation growing upwards out of undignified eighteenth-century riots, a small minority of Presbyterians in love with the vision of revolutionary France, the reaction of the Protestant majority into something inaccurately called Unionism, the drawing of a border-line to perpetuate differences in one small island . . .

The letter from Dowdall crinkled and crumpled in his pocket. The dancers danced all through Friday afternoon and Saturday morning. At least Dublin was a city; and compared with that tortured north-eastern corner of Ireland, Dublin knew its own mind. Dublin knew that it was an Irish city. A Dublin government ruled twenty six counties of the thirty-two, would in some blissful future rule the whole thirty-two. Then men would know that living together on one island bound them together with bonds stronger than the centrifugal complications of three centuries.

The paper crinkled and crumpled in his pocket, the letter from Dowdall, the invitation to a new life. The sound sent him drifting off into calm meditations, detached from the life of the town and the life of the country, with a pleasant philosophic detachment that made a man as tall as the gods. Invitation to a new life. Not for himself alone. She said she loved him. She said she would follow him into hell. The dancers danced with a splendid rhythmical elation. The music and the songs were the sweetest he had ever heard. He spent Saturday afternoon in charge of the handicraft exhibition, really interested in curios that would normally have bored him to warm, bitter, bloody tears. There were some words that could really change the world.

Maybe it was selfish. Davy was somewhere and Davy was almost inevitably in trouble. But what in hell could one do about Davy? Davy was incorrigible. Davy had got himself into trouble. Davy had been reasonably clear of danger, and had returned into danger because he wanted to make himself a thorough nuisance. Peter wiped his conscience clean, walked on Sunday morning through the splendid autumn sunlight to the field by the tennis courts where the festival would conclude. The paper crinkled and crumpled in his pocket. The world was a new world, jubilant with sunlight.

The town was crowded. The field was crowded. People crowded along the pavements from the town to the field. Bands blared, drummed, piped, jangled, fluted down the wide flat stretch between the gate and the broad field. There were sideshows, tea tents, stalls with coloured bottles and coloured foods, all the stage properties that went with gay, light-hearted, inconsequential joy. Peter and Rita entered into it without reserve.

"Diogenes was a fool," said he. "Diogenes at the fair."

"What did he do?" asked Rita.

"Went around wearing a barrel," said Jim Carson. "Like poor papa."

"Not quite. When he saw the rustics enjoying themselves he went away thanking the gods there were so many things Diogenes could do without."

"Maybe he was right," said Carson. "Maybe they were nasty rustics. I've seen carry-on at hiring-fairs that I wouldn't like to have my name associated with."

He guffawed at some secret joke. They sat with Arty Williams in a group on the grass near the edge of the water. Jack and Mary passed that way, joined the group.

"This is quite a party," said Carson.

"Except for Davy," said Mary.

"Davy's all right," said Arty Williams. "He'll manage. Nobody will bother about him across the border. After a while the whole thing will be forgotten. Slevin's the man they want."

Somebody else echoed: "Slevin's the man they want." And then suddenly they were silent looking out on the wide field where the people crowded around the touchline waiting for the county football match that would bring to a finish the three festive days.

"If we could only go back," said Mary, "to the time before all this trouble happened. Poor Davy. What came over him?"

"He acted with the best intentions, Mary," said Williams.

"I know. But he got into trouble just the same. Good intentions aren't everything."

"It was hard on his father and mother," said Carson. "But it never was a disgrace in this country to get on the wrong side of the police. It might have been any of us. Look at all the young fellows in Belfast gaol. No accusation. No trial. Nothing but gaol."

"The system is at fault," said Jack.

"Anyway," said Carson, "there's no cause to worry. Davy's well away from here."

Peter listened and said nothing. He had told no one that Davy had voluntarily abandoned his safety, because he was afraid they might awkwardly guess at Davy's reasons. He looked fixedly at the field where people had suddenly commenced cheering, welcoming the appearance of the rival teams. A brass band went before the double line of active, jerseyed men. They stood to attention in the centre of the field. Everybody stood to attention. The band played "The Soldiers' Song." The green, white and gold tricolour was hauled to the top of the flagstaff. Somebody sang: *Soldiers are we, whose lives are pledged to Ireland.*

"It might have been any of us," said Peter.

"Peter, you're sneering," said Mary.

"This is Ireland, Peter," bellowed Carson. "We acknowledge no border. We are one people. The indomitable Irishry."

"I know," said Peter. "The blood of the martyred generations moves within you when you hear that tune. You see Pearse, Plunkett, Connolly. The burning post office in Dublin in 1916. Eamonn de Valera in Boland's mills, declaring for freedom with a hot rifle and a barricade of bags of flour."

"Not an accurate picture. What do you see, Peter?"

"The empty place at home where Davy should sit. The work he should do for his father and mother."

"He's not the first man to be driven from his home. He won't be the last."

"What for? A dead man and stolen money in a village street."

"Don't blame Davy. Don't blame Ireland. Don't blame the hope that generations of Irishmen have guarded with their blood."

"Then I blame the English. Or the Orangemen. No, Jim, it won't do. There must be some other real way of solving our problems. Our real problems."

"For example?"

"Not whether a stupid borderline divides one small island. But whether men of goodwill can smash down the spiritual border that divides the people."

"You'd go a long way in an Orange lodge, Peter, with that argument." Carson shook with laughter. "Or in Downing Street. New hope for English politicians. New light for the sons of William. We are all brothers under the skin."

His laughter was lost in the wild cheering of the crowd. The game was on.

"I'm thirsty," said Jim Carson. "Come on, Peter. We'll forage for the camp."

They went across the grass towards one of the stalls. A thirsty crowd swayed and milled around the wooden counter, reached eagerly for bottles of insipid minerals. Peter halted hesitantly on the fringe of the struggle.

"No future in that," he said.

"Watch me," said Carson. He rushed into the struggle, shouldered and elbowed his way until the gapped wall of human bodies closed again behind him and he was lost from sight. Peter waited leisurely. All the minerals ever gassed wouldn't be worth such a hullabaloo. The crowd swayed to the right and the left, shouting and laughing, enjoying the fun. Then another gap opened and a girl leaped out triumphantly grasping a bottle of lemonade in each hand. She straightened up, drew a long, satisfied breath of triumph, saw Peter and recognised him.

"Hello, Josie," he said.

"I want you for a minute," she whispered. Her air of smiling triumph had changed to one of quiet, determined conspiracy. The two yellow bottles were suddenly very incongruous. He followed her round to the back of the stall, away from the shouting crowd, out of sight of the field.

"If anybody sees us here," she said, "they'll be jumping to conclusions."

"Let them jump. You've something on your mind, Josie?"

"Have I something on my mind." Great America once again spoke in the rising nasal note. "I know where your brother is. I have a message from him."

"Where is he?"

"Dick Slevin said I wasn't to tell that. I know Dick Slevin. He sneaked into the back o' the shop last night when the boss an' the missus were at the pictures."

"Then they're in the town?"

"It's a fair guess."

"They're mad fools."

"You're tellin' me."

"What was the message?"

"It wasn't for you. I don't want to make you jealous. But Slevin said your brother wanted to see Miss Keenan. As soon as possible. Slevin said your brother was cracked. I don't want to approach her. But I couldn't tell that to Slevin."

"I'll do it for you, Josie," He gripped her arm, enforcing the meaning of his words with a gentle pressure that made the saucy eyes smile up at him with comradely understanding.

"Do, you know the dance hall behind Keenan's house?'

"Who doesn't?"

"Could Davy get up there without anybody seeing him?"

"Your brother. He could."

"Could you get a message to him now?"

"I could try."

"Good." He patted her shoulder. "Run to it, Josie. When you've lowered that lemonade. Miss Keenan will be there waiting."

He slipped out from behind the stall to witness the emergence of Jim Carson, dishevelled, red-faced, perspiring, but gloriously clutching an armful of coloured bottles. He took his share of the bottles, led the way back to their party. The solid backs of the people cut off all view of the football match. Boots thumped on the bouncing ball. Cheering began hesitantly, swelled like a rising flood as the play swept up and down the field. They sipped lemonade; They chatted casually about a thousand things. The river-water danced past, liberated from the town, liberated from the last bridge. On the far bank of the river a few soldiers gathered in a group on a small hillock to follow the movement of the game. All around them was the flat spread of green holm, circled by the wide sweep of the river. Towering above them was the grey barracks, and behind the barracks the spires and the highest roofs of the town. Peace was there, the autumn sun, the pigeons drooling lazily above narrow sunny streets. By the river there was festival and shouting, people crowding for coloured bottles. They sipped lemonade. They chatted casually about a thousand things. Peter watched his chance to catch Rita's eye, to get her apart from the crowd. She would go to meet Davy. Peter would go to meet Davy. Together they would talk sense into him. They would settle the business once and for all.

VI

Josie made her excuses to her two girl-friends. She said the sun had given her a headache. She knew they wouldn't offer to go with her because a crowd meant men, and they wanted men. The long straight road that led up to the town was empty and quiet. The streets were quiet. There were so many people in the field by the river. A young policeman looked after her as she went up the hill by the courthouse. She tried to convince herself that he knew where she was going, tried to feel like Veronica Lake sent on a secret and mysterious mission, hair down over one eye, her body slim in one of those long glossy dresses. But Josie knew in her heart that the young policeman was looking after her legs, her neat body neatly enclosed in a new green costume, her natural blond hair. She was proud of her legs, her soft rubber-soled shoes, her hair, her new costume. But she wasn't flattered by the swivelling movement of the policeman's eyes. Policemen weren't in her line. She raised her head disdainfully and walked on.

The door of the shop was closed. The boss and the missus and that awful child were off for the day in the country. Josie fished the key out of her handbag, let herself into the quiet, empty house, closed the door carefully behind her, testing the firmness of the lock, once, twice, three times. Once again she was Veronica Lake: walking up the echoing floor, between the empty snugs, with a step and movement that did not naturally belong to her; posing before the fly-marked mirror that hung behind the counter. Then she laughed suddenly at her own affected gait, at her reflection posing back at her out of the mirror. Veronica Lake was paid big money for pretending to do that sort of thing. Josie Blaney did the real thing and what did she get for it? A friendly pat on the shoulder. A half-hearted kiss, given with his mind on somebody else, on that Keenan girl. It was a pity. He was a nice fellow. Just a little bit out of her way. If she had met him somewhere else she might have gone for him.

But not here in the town where everybody knew everything about everybody else. She was still leaning on the counter, all the laughter and posture drained out of her, leaning quietly on the counter and watching her own quiet reflection in the fly-marked mirror.

What did she get for it? What did she get for it? She thumped out the words down the long wooden steps, down into the wilderness of sheds and outhouses, rusty zinc, tarred timber, dull brick, that fringed the Red Lion yard. If the boss found out, she got the sack. If the police found out? They couldn't put her in gaol. What good would that do them? They wouldn't bother their eyebrows. A boy in trouble was a boy in trouble. His brother too.

She stopped at the door of a high brick storehouse, fished another key out of her handbag, opened the padlock that fastened the door. One consolation was that she had that Slevin fellow under lock and key. He couldn't move without her permission, couldn't sneak into the shop to pester her when there was nobody else about. He hadn't been pleased, but there was only one key and no way of fastening a padlock on the inside of the door. So Dick Slevin had been compelled to do what he was told, for once in his life. Going up the ladder to the loft she thought that maybe, if Dick Slevin's mother had given him the stick good and proper, he wouldn't be in trouble himself, wouldn't have dragged the other poor fellow into trouble. Slevin wanted a hammering, a good hammering. She straightened up in the dim loft. She couldn't stand the sleeky cheek of the fellow, the nerve of him, thinking himself another James Cagney.

She called softly: "Davy, Davy Quinn."

It was dangerous. Still, the boss trusted her, didn't often visit the store himself. Anyway, the place was as high and big as the workhouse.

She called again: "Davy. Davy Quinn."

"I'm here. What is it?"

"We're both here," said Dick Slevin's voice. "Have you brought us a free pardon, blondie?"

She tightened her lips. She said: "Davy Quinn, I'm talking to you."

"I'm listening, Jose."

"That one will see you in the dance hall."

"When?"

"Right away."

"Will there be nobody to see me?" asked Slevin.

"You stay where you are."

"I am nobody's darling. Listen, Josie, take me over to the shop and make me a cup of tea."

"Oh, go to hell."

"Please, Josie. We're bloody well choked with dust."

Above her head a pair of legs came dangling out of the shadows, swayed for a moment with a pendulous motion; then Davy dropped down from the little lightless attic that filled the ridge of the roof. Slevin followed him. They stood up, brushed their untidy clothes, blinking their eyes like men who had been for a long time without light.

"As dark as a bag up there," said Davy.

"What do you want—searchlights?"

"No offence, Josie. It was decent of you to take us in. I still can't understand why you bothered your head about us."

"Your natural sex appeal," said Slevin.

She turned on Slevin. "It wasn't yours, anyway, squinty." Then she was sorry for her anger, seeing Slevin's tired, crestfallen face, mentally promising him that cup of tea.

"We won't trouble you much longer, Josie," said Davy. "We can jump the old goods train this evening. It'll be safe. The town's quiet, isn't it?"

He led the way down the ladder, slipped cautiously out and disappeared around the corner of the building. For a hundred yards he was sheltered by the irregular jumble of sheds and outhouses. To his right hand was the dusty, grass-spotted expanse of the Red Lion yard, sloping gently upwards to the top of the railway cutting. Behind him in the distance were the great white gates through which carts and lorries passed in and out. The gates were closed. The shadows of the houses lengthened over the empty, deserted place. Josie caught a glimpse of him as he ran across the empty space separating him from the steps that led up to the dance hall. He ran with his shoulders hunched, with a peculiar sideways step as if his right shoe were hurting him. She felt pain like a sudden blow deep down in her body, a desire to mother somebody. Slevin stood beside her, quiet and patient, with no quick remarks on his tongue. He said: "One little cup, Josie. You'd give it to a dog."

She said: "Our dog doesn't drink tea." But she gave him the key of the padlock all the same. She said: "Follow me in ten minutes. Make sure that nobody sees you." She thumped up the long wooden steps. Her feet hammered out: "What did she get for it?" But she wanted to take the whole world to her heart, all the people that were in trouble, all the people that were miserable. She had enough warmth there to do the whole world good.

VII

Davy raced up the stone steps, across the narrow cobbled yard. The door of the dance hall was open and he was over the threshold like a flash. Peter and Rita stood by a window, their backs to the door. Davy's hand smoothed down his wiry black hair, scraped the stubble on his square chin. He kicked the door shut behind him and walked slowly across the floor.

"I wanted to see you, Rita," he said.

"I came along," said Peter.

"I've got nothing to talk to you about."

"But I've got something to talk to you about."

Peter crossed to the door, turned the key in the lock, put the key carefully into his pocket.

"Now, Davy," he said, "I'm going to talk some quick talking. For Rita and myself. For your own welfare."

"You're so decent."

"Well, if you won't have sense yourself, somebody must teach you to have it."

"Big brother Peter."

"Shut up, Davy. Shut up and listen to me."

Peter was standing beside Davy. Peter's face was white with anger. Rita standing by the window watched nervously. Davy sighed resignedly, once again smoothed his stiff hair, sat down on the edge of the band platform.

"I don't know exactly what you want to see Rita about. But I can make a rough guess. And I'm going to deal with that point first. Rita and I are going to be married. We were in love with each other when you had nothing in your head but the freeing of poor old Mother Ireland."

Davy opened his mouth to interrupt.

"Now, wait a minute. That's one point settled. We'll get on to the next. Davy, you've been behaving like something between a child and a lunatic. When you were in safety you hadn't the common gumption to stay there. What do you think the old people will feel like when they hear that you've come back? At the best you'll finish up in gaol."

"I'd be out of your way then."

"I don't want you out of the way. I just want you to have a bit of common sense. Whether you're here or anywhere else doesn't make any difference to me . . . to us."

"I came here to talk to Rita."

"Talk to her, then. Ask her what she thinks about it all. I've said everything I can say."

Davy stood up and walked towards Rita. She still stood with her back to the window, her hands gripping the sill, her face very pale and very tired. He held her gently by the shoulder. Over the red metal bridge he could see a long line of soldiers marching three deep. Their movement was curiously pantomimic like a movie picture with sound suddenly gone dead.

"Rita," he said, "do you remember that night, long ago, in this place? The ghosts. You remember—the place, you said, was haunted."

She nodded her head.

"Do I know now, Rita, what you meant?"

Her voice was very low. She said: "Yes, Davy."

"And you really do love Peter?"

"Yes, Davy."

"And you've always loved him?"

"Yes, Davy."

He smiled. His eyes had a childish, woebegone light of understanding, fading into dull realisation of pain. She knew then why she could have married Davy. She knew why she loved and why she would marry Peter. They were brothers, resembling each other somewhere deep down in the soul. In them their mother's faded patience had been transformed into a gentle, manly pity; their father's aged pettishness into Peter's quiet pride, into Davy's shock-headed, pig-headed stubbornness. They were brothers in blood and bone, and in spirit; and she had come between them, driving them apart. She led Davy across the floor. She stood between them, holding an arm of each.

"It's my fault," she said. "Let us have peace, Peter and Davy. I'm not worth quarrelling over."

"Quarrelling !" said Davy. "You're worth fighting a war for."

And suddenly the two brothers joined hands and laughed together. She didn't laugh. She said seriously: "I've caused a lot of trouble. Nothing's worth fighting a war over."

Peter saw the long, bewildered lines on the exploding beaches, the planes screaming in the air, the guns at sea, the guns on the land, the terrified people crowding along wrecked roads. Davy saw the advance of goose-stepping feet, rhythmical, beautiful, as graceful as some sweeping classical dance.

"You've been listening too much to Peter," said Davy. "He's a class of a pacifist."

"He's wise."

"Pacifism never solved anything. The gun solves the problem. Just read the history of this country and see how far we ever got with peace politics or parliamentary palaver. Wasn't it the Fenians that . . ."

Rita laughed suddenly, her arms around Davy's shoulders, shaking him as a child would shake a doll or a teddy-bear, or a mother shake an incorrigible, lovable child.

"If Jack were here," said Peter, "he would say: 'Davy Quinn, Radical, revolutionary and Irish Republican'."

"I'd like to see Jack," said Davy. "And Mary. How is she?"

"Mary's well," said Rita. "She's going to have a baby."

"Cheers, Peter. We'll be uncles. How do the . . . old people take the news?"

"It's a new life for them. They don't worry any more now. When they feel that you're safe out of harm's way . . ."

Davy moved suddenly. "God, I nearly forgot. Slevin will be waiting. The goods train."

He walked quickly to the door. "You two stay here. Give me ten minutes to get clear. We'll be across the border in an hour's time."

"Shake off Slevin then as soon as you can. He's no good. He'd get you into trouble in heaven."

"I will, Peter."

He opened the door slightly, turned around to look at them, swallowed slowly and painfully.

"I wish you luck then. The two of you. Remember me to everybody."

She went across to him and kissed him. He smiled with a pathetic appearance of delighted daring.

"There y'are now. I'm not beaten yet. You better watch your step, Peter."

He went out quickly. They stood apart, silently watching the blank surface of the door. He ran across the cobbled yard, halted suddenly at the top of the stone steps. Alec MacCabe, halfway up the steps, stopped his lumbering progress, his huge body blocking the narrow passage. They stared at each other. Alec's dark eyes wrinkled and blinked. He said mechanically: "Is the boss up there?" He advanced a few steps upwards, shouted suddenly: "Heavenly Father! It's Quinn the I.R.A. man," came hopping up the steps at a speed that was stupendous for a clumsy, heavily built man. Davy timed his ascending approach, kicked out with all his force, felt his foot plunge into the soft stomach with a force that wrenched his ankle, sent him staggering backwards to the round, clean cobbles. Then the big man was doubled up, lying halfway down the steps, screaming with pain. Running footsteps approached the bottom of the steps. Davy ran—up the yard, through the long hallway, out into the street. He put his head down and ran, hammering along the cooling footpath. Nothing mattered now but speed. A lounger at a street corner shouted: "Go on, Steve." A girl whistled and clicked her tongue ironically. He passed the courthouse and the barracks. A policeman idling in the door of the barracks, his hands deep in the pockets of his trousers, came to a sudden interested life, went running back down a passage into the dayroom. Davy ran down the hilly street to the shop where Josie worked. The door was closed.

In the kitchen behind the shop they heard his quick, excited knocking. Slevin put his teacup down suddenly, upsetting the tea over the table. Josie ran down the shop to the door.

"Who is it?"

"Davy. Quick, Josie. I was spotted."

"I knew it," 'said Slevin. "The bloody fool." Slevin stood behind the counter, a gun in his hand, a second gun lying on the stained, sticky surface.

"Leave it closed, Josie. Let him stay out to hell."

"He'll be caught."

"He'll only get gaol. I'll get the rope. Let him stay out, I tell you. Keep him there until I get across the yard to the railway."

Slevin's face was pale. He raised the gun, threatening her. She looked at him steadily, then spat with cool venom on the floor of the shop, and opened the door. She didn't close it again. She stood looking out into the street. Davy leaned against the counter, gasping for breath.

"Run, Dick," he said. "The railway."

"Take a gun," said Slevin. "You've fixed us good and proper. You bloody fool."

"Josie," said Davy. "The door."

She turned and surveyed them calmly. She said: "Get out. For God's sake get out. Isn't it bad enough to lose a job? You don't want to see me on the scaffold."

She looked out again, up and down the street. A dozen curious people had gathered on the opposite footpath. Windows and doors opened. Inquiring heads looked out. A policeman came running down the hill, and then another, and then another.

They clumped down the wooden steps, Davy in the lead, a gun in his fist. As he held it, it might have been a tin whistle or a Christmas candle. He didn't know for certain how the thing had got into his hand. The metal was cold and clammy against his palm. He only knew that he had to run across the yard, up the slope to the top of the cutting, to meet the goods train that was steaming out of the station. As they reached the bottom of the steps they heard the shrill whistle of the engine. They bent low and ran.

Alec MacCabe was propped up sitting against the wall in the cobbled yard behind Keenan's. A thin trickle of blood ran down from his sagging underlip, over his wide stubbled chin, dripping on to his white collar. He couldn't speak. Rita mopped his cold, perspiring face. A few men stood around and waited for the coming of the ambulance. One of the two policemen took Peter aside, produced notebook and pencil. He said: "We'll want your statement, Peter Quinn, you know."

"Yes, I know."

The other policeman leaned on the low wall and looked out over the Red Lion yard, seeing, in the blank moment that precedes perception, two running figures like two flies dancing in the sun. Then he called out suddenly and went leaping down the stone steps. Slevin saw him, heard him shout the order to halt. Slevin fired wildly. The bullet screamed off somewhere into the empty air.

Peter mechanically, answering questions heard the thud of the policeman's heavy Webley.

Rita held a glass of brandy to Alec MacCabe's lips, moistened the sweaty face with a damp cloth. The questioning policeman dropped his notebook and pencil, went racing down the cobbles, jumping down the steps, running across the yard to the place where Davy Quinn went down on his face, stiffening fingers grasping at life, grasping at the dusty naked earth.

Slevin cleared the body with a flying leap, went at full speed up the slope, shot over the edge of the cutting. The train went past with a shriek of steam. The next stop was thirteen miles up the line.

Rita held the glass to Alec MacCabe's lips. She didn't need to stand up. She didn't need to walk to the top of the stone steps and look down. She knew what had happened. She knew.

Peter picked up the notebook and pencil. He read out what the policeman had written down. It was queer to read out one's own words, written down like that in a strange book in a strange hand.

7

The Train

HIS father and Rita left him to the station. The platform was crowded with soldiers going up to Belfast, civilians going to Dublin for the weekend. They pushed their way through the crowd, found a position near the edge of the platform, found a seat in the corner of a carriage when the train had thundered into the station. Peter squeezed his bag on to the rack, leaned out of the carriage window. His father reached out his hand.

"Good-bye, son," he said. "God bless you. Take good care of yourself. Your mother will be praying for you. You're all she has now."

He went along the platform towards the exit, very small and suddenly feeble. His black suit was tight and shiny across the shoulders. At the bookstall he turned and waved his hand. They waved in return and didn't speak for a minute. Then she said: "I'll walk over with him, Peter. You'll be all right."

"Yes, Rita. I'll be all right."

They shook hands. The carriage behind them was crowded. People still crowded along the platform.

"You'll write soon?"

"Yes. I'll write soon. Keep reminding Mary to send me a letter. She's a poor hand at writing."

Their hands were still clasped. He pressed her fingers. She flushed slightly. She said: "Let's know how you like it."

"I'll like it all right. It's one way of living."

"Good luck, Peter."

"Good luck, Rita."

She passed the bookstall without looking back. He sat down and opened a book. The printed lines were very far away, irregular and indistinct. An A.T.S. girl in the seat opposite surveyed him with interest. The shabby houses with their intimate backyards dropped behind; the wide road leading to the fresh country; the bare expanse of the Red Lion yard; the spires; the irregular line of roofs; the bungalows and big houses on the edge of the town; the river drifting lazily through flat fields. A mist of rain blew down at them from a low sky, blowing across the tired autumn countryside. Somewhere along this line Dick Slevin had dropped from the train and vanished into the green wildness of fields, taking his luck with him to trouble some other townland. They never would capture Slevin. The devil's children. . . .

But then, why blame Slevin? Slevin hadn't killed Davy. The present hadn't killed Davy. His death-warrant had been written in the past, hundreds of years ago, when some passing, momentary notion crystallised into an idea, became an ideal, a vision, a dream to trouble for ever the minds of the young. The policeman raising his heavy Webley was only an instrument, as soulless as the dull black cloth of his uniform. The beauty of the vision and the dream crashed down to the earth, and there was only the body of a poor foolish boy huddled in ugly, sudden death. What good did it do to anyone? One violent death, a million violent deaths, because the notion of some one man, dead for centuries, had grown to an ideal, a vision, a dream.

The rain strengthened, whipped with fury against the windows, drew a dark curtain across the wilderness of green fields. Behind the curtain were hundreds of homes, quiet places where men lived on their own land. It was a notion, a vision, a dream that had given poor men such freedom. It was some wonderful vision that had first taught men the necessity of such freedom. Maybe the death of a foolish boy went in some obscure way to make that vision more clear and more beautiful for all men. The train whistled its way out of the track of the rain, crashed through a small halt where the sun was shining again, and a cart laden with shining creamery cans stood idle on the road outside the station. The fields were fresh after the rain. The fields were triumphant and content in the heel of the harvest.

He had promised to write to her. He would write to them and tell them how he was getting on, how he liked the job, how he liked living in the city. He would describe the new friends he made, mention the pictures and plays he saw. They would write and tell him about life in the town and, reading their letters, he would see the old, narrow, hilly streets, the ridged roofs, the limping spires, the river, the blue circle of hills. He was bound to her that way, for ever and ever... sunny afternoons, pigeons wheeling in the still air. At holiday time he would see her and they would go walking together, keeping their conversation and their minds and their eyes away from the grass-spotted dust of that awful yard. There would always be something lying there, huddled with neck and shoulders bent, arms stiff, bloody fingers dug into the ground in the sudden convulsions of pain. Death could be a terrible thing, and death had come so suddenly on the whole world, on land, on the sea, shrieking and screaming in the air. Maybe some day they would take courage and walk again across that place, think of it and speak of it as something sad but no longer horrible. On that day they would know peace. The divided peoples of the world would know peace. Their healing would be the shadow of the world's healing, as their sorrow shadowed the world's sorrow.

At Goraghwood a policeman went up the train inspecting identity cards. Two military policemen followed, examining military passes; then customs men poking in baggage, embarrassing ladies. The great plain went out beyond Newry town to the Mourne Mountains and the sea. The beautiful things of the world were forgotten. And scarring and marking that beauty was a barrier dividing Irishmen from Irishmen, symbolising the strife of the spirit that was the creation of three centuries of persistent misunderstanding. And marking the beauty of the world were barriers and barriers dividing man from man, nation from nation, laying whole countrysides waste, levelling cities, wrecking families and homes. Borders here, there and everywhere; a dead body lumped grotesquely on the dusty ground; ugly, terrible death everywhere as the end to all division and bitterness between man and man. Maybe some day Ireland would learn. Maybe some day the world would learn. Maybe....

The train rattled down through the Gap of the North, mystic country, fairy country, turn a stone and uncover a legend or a myth. Cuchullain the demigod to O'Hanlon the Rapparee and highwayman giving their ghosts to those moors and mountains and little fields. At Dundalk a clerical student got into the train, stumbled awkwardly to the one empty seat, concealed himself bashfully behind a learned periodical. Peter studied his long legs, his square-toed honest shoes; saw them walking on through the years, year after year, the chapel, the study hall, the refectory, slowly and nervously up the steps to the altar. He saw them walking to their mission, maybe in a lecture hall or classroom, to a parish in an Irish city or an Irish town, to a parish in the Irish countryside where so much that was valuable remained and would remain as long as the grass was green, where so much was needed to give life the full circle that would make happy men. Possibly the mission might be to England or Scotland or France, Africa or China or Borneo . . . a photograph in a missionary magazine . . . a grave in some forgotten corner of the earth. It was one way of living and one way of dying, and a very good way. But then it could not obviously be every man's way; going always in a triangle from the confessional where sins were forgiven to the pulpit where the word of God was preached, then slowly up the altar to something that had saved and divided men for two thousand years.

The long legs crossed and recrossed. The square toes were erect with defiant honesty, the face was hidden bashfully behind a learned magazine.

Outside the window there was flat land again and the blue sea, long grass growing lush right down to the edge of the sand, little towns, tiny harbours, long strands. Then suddenly there was a wide road of square, white modern houses; and beyond them the Hill of Howth standing out bravely against the rolling force of the water. Then the fields were gone and there were houses and spires, and to the left the ugly arms of the quayside.

Dowdall was on the platform. They went down the steep steps to the footpath, walked up Talbot Street towards Nelson's Pillar. Dowdall carried Peter's bag, swerved in and out to avoid collisions, stopped to look after a high-heeled, yellow-legged, red-coated girl. He said: "What lines, Peter. What lines. I feel stronger now."

They crossed O'Connell Street and found a cafe. Nelson on his pillar bent his one stone eye on Smith O'Brien the silk-hatted rebel, on Dan O'Connell the demagogue.

"The place is small," said Dowdall. "But it's clean. And the staff know me. They'd do anything for me. That is, almost anything. There are limits, you know."

"There are."

"I mean emergency regulations. No butter with lunch and it is illegal to serve wheaten bread or something like that."

Peter laughed at him. They consulted the menu. A girl took their order, smiled familiarly on Dowdall.

"I missed that, you know," said Dowdall, "when we used to get up at five-thirty-five. It was chilling, you must admit."

"It was."

"The time at home has done you good, Peter. You're more like a human being now. Dublin will make you a demigod. Wait and see. You'll love it. I love it. The only civilised spot in this country."

They commenced eating. The tables were green; the walls were green; the lights were green . . . a soft green that soaked into brain and body, filled the soul with the contentment of green fields. The glass revolving-door spun around and around. People came in and people went out. Through the wide window they watched the traffic go up and down the street.